Glenn!

To Jur At last!

20/5/18

HANDBRAKE PUBLISHING

ISBN 978-1-9997760-0-8

For Freddie

Thank You &
Acknowledgements

No book is a solo effort. Even if the author does most of the work, there are always others needed to get it to market in a consumable state.

Without the input, inspiration, guidance, support, encouragement, cajoling and effort of the following people, this would still be at the "good idea" stage. I am indebted to those who provided early feedback on the manuscript (Andrew Long and Helen Gallagher). Patrick Meharg for helping me find my true writing style and for his marvellous illustrations and interpretations of the characters. Sarah Howard-Coles for inspiring the original character name of Felicity. Vicki Fuller for allowing me to use her son's name. Mary Thomson for the honesty and wisdom of her advice and steering me in the right direction to get the book published in a way that was suited to my needs.

All the staff at Handbrake Publishing – you're an amazing crew.

Last and very much not least, to my wonderful and gorgeous partner Liz for helping me create the characters that populate the book, for allowing some of the dafter ideas to surface to become key elements of the story and for believing in me to get it right. Without her tireless and unwavering support, this would not have happened.

And thank you dear reader for purchasing the book in whatever format you have. There will be many more Felicity stories to come.

Glenn Coe
September 2017

Prologue

It was warming up to be a beautiful summer's morning at the Ministry of Sleep. That wasn't its real name of course. The honey coloured Cotswold stone manor house had been built 200 years ago by Joshua Turner, a wealthy local wool merchant. As was often the case in times gone by, the upkeep became too expensive for the Turner family so with the breakout of war, they were relieved when it was used as a hospital for wounded soldiers. It then stayed under Government control for a number of years during peace time. Eventually they had to sell it to an American medical insurance company who kept the family name in *'The Joshua Turner Memorial Institute for Advanced Research into Sleep Problems in Children'*. As that was a bit of a mouthful, everyone who worked there today, and all the locals, still called it simply *'The Ministry'*.

The school holidays were in full swing and the gentle sounds of an English country summer floated through the air. The bees buzzed busily from flower to flower, their legs laden with the nectar that would eventually become honey. The birds chirped merrily from the branches of the trees in the Ministry's extensive, well-kept gardens. Swifts and swallows swooped and screeched as they devoured the insects whose sound was faintly audible in the late afternoon sunshine. Everywhere was peaceful in this quiet corner of the Cotswolds – no

distant rumble of traffic, no whining of jet engines overhead and no throbbing music from far away sound systems pumping out their boring bass rhythms. It would be hard to imagine a more perfect scene.

Deep inside the Ministry building, in her small office at the end of a long shadowy corridor, Nursey Corners was restless. It was something of a tradition that staff at the Ministry were not called by their real name but by something that described what they did. Nursey Corners got her nick-name because of her insistence that all the sheets in the beds had to be tightly tucked in just as they were in hospitals. She was perfectly happy with this arrangement as her full name of Angelina Twissleton-Smythe made her sound a lot more *'posh'* than she really was. But having married the rather dashing young Guards Captain, Jonny Twissleton-Smythe, when she was only 21, this became her new surname.

Nursey was head of the Sleep Walking section where she worked closely with her rather crumpled but well-meaning assistant Lottie. Having made her morning rounds and finding Lottie unusually grumpy, she immediately noticed Lottie's rather evasive, almost shifty, manner.

Something was clearly troubling her as she gazed out of the open window overlooking the garden. Nursey had already spotted the trail of footprints leading to and from the dormitory and determined to put Lottie on the spot to see what she might be covering up.

'All present and correct Lottie?' Nursey's voice took the rather distracted Lottie by surprise.

Lottie Lightbulb, as she was inevitably known because she worked in the section responsible for children who had to sleep with a light on, was dozy in all senses. Not exactly the brightest bulb in the chandelier.

'Oh yes ma'am. Everything's fine,' she replied but the shifty look in her eye and the way she shuffled her feet said otherwise.

'Got you,' thought Nursey to herself. 'Now I know you're fibbing.'

'Hmmm, if that is the case Lottie, how then do you explain the muddy foot prints in the hall way next to the dormitory?' asked Nursey, fixing Lottie with a steely stare.

Lottie's mouth opened and closed a few times before any words came out.

'I expect the girls forgot to wipe their feet before coming in Ma'am. You know what them youngsters is like' stuttered Lottie, desperately hoping that Nursey would be thrown off the scent. She should have known better by now.

Nursey was used to getting information from people who were unwilling to provide it. Her years of training cadets in the Army had taught her that and her patience with those unwilling to co-operate, or who thought they could deceive her, was very low.

'Well Lottie they were muddy *bare* footprints, and more than one set, if the different sizes are anything to go by. So that rather scuppers your theory, doesn't it?' retorted Nursey. 'Unless of course you nodded off during the night?'

'I didn't fall asleep I promise. I was awake the whole night and put the music on just as you told me,' wailed Lottie.

`So how did these girls manage to sneak out and back in again, past your office, if you were as alert as you say?' Nursey persisted, sensing that Lottie had something to hide. `Are you SURE you heard and saw nothing Lottie? Nothing at all out of the ordinary that would explain how these girls managed to get outside?'

`I didn't hear or see a thing ma'am. I don't know how it happened or who done it. I checked all the doors and the CCTV – there was nothing. Maybe it was just kids from the village having a prank?'

Lottie offered this explanation in the vain hope that Nursey would be persuaded to look somewhere other than Lottie. Fat chance. Nursey's instinct was to mistrust all information she was given and to verify it for herself. She looked at Lottie for a few moments to see if she would add anything.

`I'm certain ma'am – it's a complete mystery to me. I would hate it if anything nasty happened' Lottie blurted out. Nursey softened her tone a little as she could see that Lottie too was a little distressed.

`If that is the case Lottie, then we'll have to look further. A LOT further. I won't have muddy children traipsing in and out of my dorm when they feel like it. Anything could happen to them once they are outside at night. Good heavens girl, what would the parents think of us if one of them was harmed in our charge?'

'No ma'am, er, I mean, yes ma'am. You're right of course.' Lottie hoped that by agreeing with Nursey she would be let off the hook. Nursey reached out and put her hand on Lottie's shoulder to reassure her.

'It is indeed a mystery as you say Lottie. One we have to get to the bottom of, and quickly. With top security at our disposal, how on earth would a few youngsters from the village two miles away get out of bed at night, scale the four-metre tall fence, dance around outside with no shoes on, bring the mud inside, and then scarper without being seen or heard?' Nursey was losing patience with the lack of information from Lottie but realized that Lottie was probably telling the truth – although Nursey was convinced that Lottie had fallen asleep at her desk.

'No ma'am, I suppose you're right. Maybe our girls were hungry? Went in search of food?' Lottie tried to make it all sound very reasonable but Nursey was unconvinced.

Naturally the children were a bit nervous at being away from home but Nursey was kindness personified when it came to dealing with the young ones in her care. A caring woman by nature she would patiently listen to each child who came to the Ministry and reassure them. Nursey Corners also believed in 'tough love' so whilst she was kind, she was also strict. Bedtime meant bedtime. Meals were taken at the table with others – no child ate alone in their room. Television was carefully rationed and all personal devices had to be left in Nursey's safe for the duration of their stay. The most important thing was that her methods worked and every child went back home with their sleep walking cured. That is why parents trusted her.

'OK Lottie, off you go, leave this with me, I can see you're tired so get some rest now and we'll review this again later today when I have poked around the grounds a bit more. There must be something to tell us where this came from and how it happened,' conceded Nursey as she could see that she wasn't going to get much more from Lottie this morning.

Lottie took the chance and turned for the door. She was almost through it when she heard Nursey's voice call after her.

'Just make sure you don't tell anyone Lottie. Not a soul, you understand? We need to get this sorted before anyone gets suspicious.'

Lottie nodded vigorously and scuttled off before Nursey could change her mind.

Nursey thought about what she had just heard and paced around her office trying to make some sense of it.

Her whole approach to curing children of their sleep walking habit relied on them not getting out of bed in the first place. She was of the firm opinion that modern duvets were to blame, and, being rather old fashioned in her views, was equally certain that by using sheets and blankets tucked into the corners of the mattress in the traditional way children would be less likely to get up and wander.

Now the revelations from Lottie threw that whole approach into doubt. She had to get to the bottom of it, and soon, as she did not trust Lottie to keep the information to herself for long. Nursey decided there and then that she had to tell her boss, the Director of the Institute, the formidable Bertrand Alexander Carrington, known to one and all at the Ministry as Bertie Bedstead. Only someone very brave, or stupid, ever dared call him that within his earshot though. In his presence, he was the 'Director'.

He too was an ex-military man but had left the Army after a stint at the Ministry of Defence. Bertie liked to talk up his `glittering military career' as if he had been some kind of war hero. But the reality was that he had never seen action and served most of his time behind a desk at the Army Pay Corps. That had not suited him at all, especially having to deal with all the paperwork. With the hint of a scandal hanging over him he was relieved when the chance came to take early retirement. The allegations about some missing money, that should have gone to caring for wounded veterans, simply refused to go away. When an offer of a cushy job in the civilian world had come from an old friend in the City, he was happy to take it. Even though he was no longer in the Army, his manner in dealing with people could still be a little sharp until he realised they did not take orders as his soldiers had done. He had managed to form a decent working relationship with Nursey though, given their shared history of being in the Army.

Once the afternoon quiet period had begun, when all the children were allowed to take a nap or read a book just as long as they didn't chatter, Nursey strode purposefully towards the Director's office past walls lined with pictures all themed around sleep. Snoring people in beds with old fashioned night caps, kittens fast asleep on cushions and of course, Sleeping Beauty, all looked down at her as she strode up to the oak panelled door of the Director's office. Normally this was his favourite time of day when he could put his feet up on his desk or stretch out on his sofa and have an uninterrupted snooze.

She pressed her ear against the cool wood and listened to see if she could tell if he was awake or asleep. The unmistakable sound of gentle snoring greeted her stifled only slightly by the thick door. Most people would have crept away again not wishing to intrude or break the Director's nap. Nursey was not most people.

Three short sharp raps on the door with her knuckles rang out into the Director's office. She could hear him jumping out of his chair and clearing his throat.

'Enter,' came the deep bellowing voice that was well used to making itself heard on parade grounds to hundreds of troops. The problem was that he used the same volume when he was talking to individuals two feet away. They soon learned to stand further back to avoid being sprayed with spit.

Nursey grasped the door knob, turned it and walked briskly in coming to the Director's desk and standing ramrod straight in front of him with her hands clasped behind her back. He probably would have preferred a salute but there was no way that would come from Nursey Corners.

'Good afternoon Bertie' she boomed, 'sorry to disturb your slumbers.' She was also the only person in the Ministry who got away with calling him Bertie – which he tolerated, just, mainly because he too was a little bit afraid of upsetting Nursey.

Nursey suppressed a wry smile. It was an open secret that the Director took a snooze each day and that he snored like a warthog.

'What brings you here on this fine summer's afternoon Nursey Corners – don't tell me one of your little darlings has escaped your clutches? He gave a nervous little giggling laugh at his own joke, risking that it would have the opposite effect on Nursey, who was ferociously defensive of her record.

'Of course not, Bertie. You know that no-one has ever done that. But I have to tell you that I am worried by some recent incidents. At first, I thought they were just isolated cases, but there is a definite pattern emerging. And I think there can only be one explanation.'

A slight nervous smile crept over the Director's face and he twirled one end of his carefully cultivated moustache thoughtfully. In his mind's eye, he thought this made him look important but to everyone else he just looked like a twit. Thoughts of his narrow escape from scandal in the Army played across his mind.

'Surely you are not telling me there is something going on here we don't know about?' he said mischievously, but very worried that there was indeed something he didn't know about yet.

'That is exactly what I am telling you Bertie.' Nursey Corners leaned forward and put her hands on his desk looking him straight in the eye.

'So, what exactly is this pattern you have observed Nursey Corners? And what do you think is the explanation?' He pushed back in his chair trying to look relaxed but he overdid it and nearly fell over, which only raised Nursey's suspicions even higher.

'I think you'd better pour yourself a stiff drink Bertie. This might take some time.' Nursey responded with both a sigh and a hint of steely determination in her voice. Once Nursey had completed her report and left the office, Bertie opened up the safe disguised behind the picture of him on the wall, took out the mobile phone he kept hidden in it and punched in a number. He heard the familiar ring tone of the French phone system. The call was answered quickly.

'Oui,' came the voice he recognised.

'You idiot,' hissed the Director, 'she's on to us. We'll have to go to our back up plan. Don't let me down this time – this is your last chance.'

'Mon dieu. OK, d'accord,' he agreed and with that the call was ended. The Director leaned back in his armchair. His mind raced through their previously agreed fall-back position. What should his next step be? He realised that time was short and he had to move quickly.

Chapter 1

Felicity Frampton gazed out through the window of their holiday caravan at the grey clouds scudding over the sea and the rain blown in on the gusts of wind. Every year they came to the same place and stayed in the same caravan for two weeks in summer. Normally the weather on the South Coast was pretty good and she was able to play outside or walk down to the beach that was part of the caravan park, with her younger brother Dougie. But today it was wet and miserable and she and Dougie had used up all the board games they brought with them.

'I'm bored,' groaned Dougie. He was an extremely active little boy and needed to be outside to burn off some of his energy. 'Can't we go outside anyway Felicity?' he pleaded, knowing full well that his sister hated the rain and getting wet.

'Yuk-a-billy,' squawked Felicity. 'I'm not going to get all wet again just for you, so you'll just have to wait until it stops. Can't you read your book or something?'

Dougie sighed a sigh that said he had already read it. Felicity ignored him and concentrated even more on what she was reading even though she'd now been over the same page several times as she too was getting restless being cooped up inside.

Felicity glanced over at her father who was sitting in the corner window seat of the caravan with the best view out over the sea. He was gazing listlessly out at the rain and clouds, and she could see he was lost in his own thoughts. Felicity knew that look. When they had been alone together he confided in her about how much he wished their mum was still alive. She would know what to do. She always did. But she had died four years ago, when Dougie was only just three years old. Poor Dougie couldn't really remember too much about her. But Felicity did and she knew her father worried that she wouldn't talk about her mother, but it was overwhelming. So she too kept her thoughts bottled up inside.

Brad Frampton had never been much of a communicator and struggled to find ways to keep his children engaged and entertained on holidays. He knew that he should probably take them somewhere else as they were getting to an age where they needed more stimulus than was available at a British holiday camp on the coast. Although they had laughed and enjoyed the pantomimes put on by the camp's entertainment team, they knew all the jokes now and it had ceased to capture their attention or imagination. He had taken the easy road again this summer and was starting to regret it. Had they gone camping in France they would have been sure of better weather, a warm pool and lots of other children to play with. He vowed this would be the last year.

'Dad...' Felicity's voice jerked him back to the caravan.

'Yes, sweet pea, what is it?' he smiled at her, seeing her mother's vivid blue eyes looking straight back at him.

'Can you come with Dougie and me to the beach when it stops raining?' she asked, her upturned little face a picture of innocence, even though her father knew she was extremely adept at getting what she wanted without apparent effort.

'Well, it is our last day here so we should try to make the most of the beach,' he agreed. 'Shall we go looking for crabs in the rock pools?' He knew they loved poking around in the pools that formed after the tide had gone out and reaching in to turn over stones that hid all manner of mysterious marine treasures.

'Oh yeah,' cried Felicity and Dougie in unison, as they both started for the door. Dougie managed to open it a crack against the wind.

'Hey Dad – it's not raining any more!' he exclaimed. 'Can we go now?'

Felicity jumped up to the window and shrieked with delight as she saw the sun poking through a break in the clouds. It had indeed stopped raining.

'Come on Dad, let's get going before it starts again,' and with that she pulled on her bright yellow waterproof jacket with the hood. It was really last year's coat, so was now a little short in the sleeves for her. She didn't mind.

Felicity was not one to worry too much about having the latest fashions or to have what everyone else had. She knew that times were a little difficult for the family and that her dad was doing everything he could to keep things as normal as possible for them. Dougie wasn't quite so aware as she was, so she just told him to accept what he got and that everything would be alright. Which it nearly always was.

Dougie almost fell out of the door in his desire to get down to the beach with his Dad. This was his favourite thing in the whole world and he wasn't going to waste a minute of it. And off they went, down the gently sloping path through the other caravans, through the gap in the white fence that marked the end of the holiday camp and down between the sand dunes to the beach.

They both ran ahead of their father who, as ever, was laden down with the nets, buckets, coats and wellies that helped protect their feet from the sharp edges of the rocks as well as providing a little bit of grip on the slimy seaweed. Even though the wind was still gusting, it was warm in the late afternoon sun and the light sparkled on the white tops of the waves. Felicity and Dougie ran to the end of the curving sandy beach just below where the rock rose from the sand into little mini cliffs. At the foot of these rock faces the sea had eroded the stone into lots of small and large pools that, with the tide out, were now full of fresh clear sea water.

'Hang on you two – wait for me,' Brad called out, but his voice was carried away on the wind and the children kept on running, playing tag as they did and trying to trip each other up. It was all done in fun of course but it always seemed to be Dougie who ended up clattering to the ground and getting covered in sand. His sister suspected he did it deliberately as he just liked doing it.

Once they got to the rocks they stopped to catch their breath and to see where their father was.

'Come ON dad,' they shouted, 'we want our nets now.'

Brad started running towards them and as he got close he dropped all their stuff and started chasing them in circles, pretending not to keep up with them. As he caught each one in turn he would pick up first Dougie and then Felicity and swing them around and around until they squealed for him to stop. They loved it of course and they kept running away from him so he would have to chase them again and again.

'OK enough – you two will wear your Dad out. Let's see what's in these pools, shall we?'

They passed the next two hours together, happily reaching into the water with bare hands to try and catch some of the small shrimp-like creatures flitting back and forth in the pools. Each giggling with delight at every new discovery and sometimes pretending to push something wet and slimy down the collar of the other. Eventually they had been through all the pools and Brad realised it was getting to tea time, which meant he would have to get something ready for their evening meal.

'Right you two – time to get back if you want to have some dinner tonight,' he stated brightly but firmly. He knew that left to their own devices, they would stay out until either darkness or exhaustion overtook them.

'Oh Dad, can't we stay a bit longer? Please….?' Dougie was first to ask, but Felicity soon added her voice.

'Sorry boys and girls but it IS getting late and we're leaving tomorrow so we will have to clean the place up as well. But tell you what, if you agree to help me with that, we can have a special treat tonight.'

'Tell us, tell us – what is it Dad. Go on, tell us…' they both chimed.

'Only if you promise to help,' he replied knowing full well they would be too tired to do it but he wanted to keep the promise he had made to his wife when she was in the last stages of her cancer that he would continue to bring them up the way they had agreed, which was they had to earn treats by doing something to help.

And so it was that they ended up in the fish and chip shop which was run by a very friendly Italian family who were always happy to have children in their café. Cod and chips all round, lashings of ketchup for the kids and a proper Italian 'Gelato' to finish. Bliss.

As the sun started to reach the horizon they got back to their caravan. Brad realised he had left his mobile phone behind and when he picked it up to see if he had missed any calls he saw that there were three calls from his sister, along with a text message asking him to ring her as soon as he could. It was unusual for his older sister to call him on his mobile so he knew that something must have happened.

He settled the children down in front of the small portable TV they had brought to the caravan and said he just had to make a call. He stepped outside for a better signal and pushed the button to speed dial his sister. She answered immediately.

'Hi Ange, what's up?' he said trying to sound nonchalant, although he was secretly a little worried. He always called her 'Ange' rather than her full name of Angelina, just as she always called him Brad. Outsiders hearing a call between, 'Brad and Angelina' usually thought it was someone else.

'Brad, I have a problem and I need your help. Actually, to be more precise, I need Felicity's help.'

'Right, I will call you when we get home tomorrow. We should be back by lunchtime, so why don't you aim to get to us about 4?'

'Perfect, I'll see you then. And Brad ...not a word to anyone yet, not even Felicity. It is vital this stays completely under wraps for now.' And with that, she rang off.

Brad went back into the caravan to find his two exhausted children fast asleep in front of the TV.

'*Looks like I'm doing the cleaning then,*' he thought to himself. But he didn't mind – they'd had a great time and it had finished on a high note. It looked like tomorrow would be an interesting day.

Chapter 2

The traffic from the South Coast to Felicity's home had been lighter than normal and they made good time. On the journey back, they played their usual car games to help pass the time. Dougie's favourite was what they called 'Stobart Snap'. Each Eddie Stobart cab had a unique name on the driver's door, usually a female name such as Rose May, which meant that it was quite a challenge to see the exact same one twice. Dougie and Felicity would shout out the names as they passed the lorry and if it was one they already knew they shouted 'snap'. The first one to shout snap got a point and five points won the game, and then they would start again. As the driver, Brad could see them coming before the kids and would call out if he spotted one approaching. They would strain their necks against the seat belts to get the first view. As each one passed, excitement, and noise, peaked until they could read the name.

They arrived home around lunch time and started to unpack whilst their dad started to prepare something to eat – fish finger sandwiches! Both were ravenous and wolfed them down greedily.

Once they had finished lunch and done the washing up (which they all did together and each had assigned tasks – Dougie dried whilst Felicity washed and Dad put things away again and wiped down), Brad said he had something to tell them. Their curiosity was immediately raised.

As it was a warm sunny day, at last, they sat outside around their small garden table.

'I had a call from Auntie Ange just before we left last night,' he started. 'She's coming to see us this afternoon.'

'Yay, great Dad – we love Auntie Ange,' Felicity enthused. Dougie nodded his head vigorously in agreement.

'She has asked Felicity to help her with a little problem she has at work. But we have to do it secretly as no-one else can know.'

Dougie looked a little unhappy at the thought his sister was getting preferential treatment from their favourite aunt. Brad noticed the drop in his shoulders and the slight down turn in his mouth.

'It's OK Dougie,' he reassured him, 'you'll get your turn. I don't know what it's about any more than you do but you know Auntie Ange would always be honest with you both so we'll just have to see what she says.'

'Is it a mystery?' asked Felicity her brow furrowed in concentration. 'I love mysteries. When I grow up I want to be a detective like you Dad.'

Before her father could respond Dougie spoke up, 'So do I Dad, I want to be a detective too.'

Brad smiled and looked at them both warmly. 'You will both get a chance, I'm sure of it, but if Auntie Ange asks for something special, then there is always a good reason. We don't know what it is yet so you will just have to be patient until she gets here.'

They were both very excited now. Not just because their aunt was coming to see them but there was also a proper mystery to be solved and THEY were going to help her.

.oᴏo.

Back at the Ministry of Sleep, Nursey Corners was mulling over the information she had shared with the Director the day before. It was highly unusual for any of the children in her charge to get out of bed once they had started the Anti Sleep Walking course. She had developed several techniques to ensure the things that triggered the actions were stopped and the habit was broken.

She knew however that just pinning children into their beds with tightly made up sheets and blankets was not enough. They needed calming down to help them to sleep so she had created a gently soothing CD which played natural sounds of waves lapping on balmy beaches, topical bird song and soothing human voices. Therefore, there was only one explanation. Someone MUST have changed something. But who? And why? What was to be gained by not fixing the sleep walking problems? More importantly, who would benefit from this?

Nursey still had this faint but unshakeable feeling, that the Director was aware of rather more than he would admit to. And she was determined to find out, as she owed it to the children in her care.

After a day to reflect on what course of action she should take, Nursey realised that she would need someone to help. Someone who could blend in and not alert any potential wrong doer to the fact that she might be on to them. She wanted and needed to have evidence.

What she really needed was someone to work under cover – literally. That meant it had to be a child as an adult would clearly be too obvious and raise too many suspicions. She couldn't really ask any of the children whose parents had paid handsomely to send them to the Ministry. For one restless and sleepless night, she wrestled with this and in the morning, the answer was staring her in the face - the photograph of Felicity and Dougie she kept by her bedside.

Of course!! It was obvious. Felicity would not be considered suspicious by the other staff or other children. She was the daughter of a detective after all and so was used to observing and reporting back. Brad had made sure of that in the way he had raised her. Dougie was a different question – he was too young and too excitable. She knew he would be disappointed but it was the only way. Instead she resolved to find a way to keep him engaged and use his incredible memory for facts and figures, dates and times.

With that clear in her mind, she climbed into her car and set off for her brother's house. It was only 30 minutes away normally, but her mind was distracted with all the questions and she missed a vital turn. Consequently, she arrived a little late, somewhat frazzled and in need of a drink.

Once they had all sat down again outside and Angelina had been given a cup of tea with her biscuit, she took a deep breath and started to speak.

'What I have to tell you all is top secret – just between us, right?'

Felicity and Dougie nodded trying to look serious but inside they were bursting to ask loads of questions. Brad felt his pulse rate rising as he wasn't sure he liked the sound of this, but he said nothing and fixed his gaze on his sister.

Angelina looked directly at Felicity as she spoke. 'I know you will have a zillion questions,' she said, 'and in good time we will have the answers but for now I need your help Felicity, as this is something only you can do.'

Dougie and Brad exchanged glances and Brad could see his son was still a little put out but he said nothing. Although Brad's initial unease was growing, he decided to let Ange continue until he knew more.

Felicity's mouth dropped open and her eyebrows arched upwards. She could hardly believe this - wow, she was 'special'. Felicity was an outwardly quiet but confident girl who just got on with things without indulging in a lot of whining or arguing. People who didn't know her mistook the quietness for her being shy or nervous. They were usually proved wrong pretty quickly.

'I need you to come to the Ministry with me and stay there with the other children for a few days. There is something going on that I don't yet understand that is causing them to sleepwalk – all of them. Can you just be like one of them and tell me what you hear and see? That's all. I don't really know what I am looking for but if you can help me I might get some clues. But you MUST promise me not to call me Auntie Ange. No-one must know we are related or that you are working for me, how can I put it, *under the covers?* At the Ministry, you must call me Nursey Corners and you must do what I say to avoid anyone getting suspicious. You might be surprised to know that people think I'm quite bossy,' she said with a smile.

'I can vouch for that' said Brad, 'you were always telling me what to do when we were kids!'

'I wasn't that bad, Brad,' his sister countered, smiling, 'was I?'

'It's always tough being the younger brother, isn't it Dougie?' laughed Brad. Dougie just pulled a face and rolled his eyes. He knew better than to start that argument again but he was pleased his dad was siding with him.

'So, what else does Felicity need to do Ange?' Brad continued. 'I sort of get that you just want her to blend in and let you know if she sees anything unusual, but if something has changed that you don't know about yet, I am a little concerned that, well, you know, I don't want anything to happen to Felicity when you're not around.' There was an awkward silence for a few moments as Brad waited for his sister to reveal more and as Felicity looked eagerly at him and then back to her aunt.

'Look, I can't say for 100% certain what is going on – if I could, I wouldn't be asking for your help. The Ministry is a very safe place Brad – it has to be. We look after other people's children for them so we are very vigilant and there are CCTV cameras everywhere. But I know how much Felicity means to you – and to me – so I promise you she will be under my care all the time.' Angelina tried to sound reassuring but she could see that Brad was still having doubts.

'How will she contact you?' asked Brad, knowing that Ange had a strict, 'no mobile phones' policy.

'I've already thought of that,' replied Angelina, 'Felicity will be able to keep the phone she has now for when she goes out but when she arrives, she can hand over this one so it looks like she is being treated like all the others.' She showed Brad another more modern phone from her handbag.

'And we'll have a secret code word if Felicity needs to see me.' Angelina paused and looked at her brother and the children. Felicity swallowed hard – she nodded vigorously still keeping her serious face even though inside she wanted to squeal with delight. Dougie looked a little crestfallen but also nodded. Brad stroked his chin for a moment, weighing up the risks against the care he knew his sister would take, as well as the opportunity for Felicity to have a little independence to do something different, that was just a bit more exciting than their normal holidays.

'OK then Ange, she can go. But at the first sign of any problem, you MUST call me, right?' stated Brad, putting on his best senior police officer voice.

Felicity's face broke into a huge grin.

'You will need to come tomorrow with your bags packed. I promise you will be completely safe and once we solve this mystery, we will all have a special celebration treat. On me.' Ange spoke directly to Felicity but also shot a glance at Brad. He was smiling.

'That's OK Auntie Ange – I mean Nursey Corners ... I will be ready and I won't let you down,' said Felicity. She could hardly believe her luck. A real mystery to be solved. She felt excited and nervous at the same time ... and a little sad that Dougie was left out. But Auntie Ange had said she would give him some part to play so that was OK. She could see it now, the headlines in the newspapers - *'Frampers of the Yard solves Mystery at the Ministry.'*

As they finished and Angelina turned to leave, Brad hugged her and whispered into her ear so that the kids could not hear. 'Please look after her Ange – I couldn't bear it if anything happened to her or Dougie.' His sister looked him in the eye and said, 'You have my word – we're family. That's all that matters.' She got back into her car and drove off without looking back.

Brad somehow knew that the next few days would not be quite as restful as he had expected.

Chapter 3

Henri DuVay stared at his phone. He could scarcely believe what the Director had just told him. They had been so careful, so meticulous in their planning. Surely there was no way there could be a problem now? But no matter how many times he went over the conversation in his head, it was clear that Nursey Corners could become a problem if not handled swiftly.

His previous dealings with the Director had been fairly straightforward but on a much smaller scale. This was the big one. This was the one that would enable him to retire to the Caribbean in style. Just as long as the Director was able to keep his end of the bargain and use his Army contacts, he could land the massive contract that would make him rich.

Despite his obvious *'Frenchness'*, DuVay had been schooled and brought up in England so he was very familiar with how things worked there and could lose his French accent in a heartbeat to pass himself off as a 'Hooray' Henri. It was time to call in some favours. He scrolled though the numbers on his phone and selected one. A familiar voice answered.

'Hello, WSB Technology, Braithwaite speaking, how may I be of assistance?'

'Wally old boy, how are you my friend? Long time, no speak. It's Henri here, Henri DuVay.'

Wally Braithwaite knew all too well who it was and groaned a silent *"eeh bah gum"* to himself. This could only mean trouble. Trouble for

Wally that was. His memory of the last encounter with the Frenchman was painfully fresh and he was in no hurry to repeat the experience.

'Oh, hello Henri, how nice to hear from you,' he lied. 'How's business in the world of duvets these days? Bit sleepy, is it?' He chortled to himself at what he thought was a clever joke, but DuVay wasn't sharing it with him.

'Well Wally, it would probably be a lot better if you hadn't let me down so badly but you know me. I don't hold a grudge. Business is business eh? Always look forwards I say.'

'Indeed Henri, couldn't agree more. So, what is it you're looking forward to if I may be so bold? And where, exactly, do I fit in?' Wally was well aware that Henri would only be calling him if he needed something.

'I'm glad you asked that Wally and I am pleased to hear you are willing to help me. You know I hate to ask and it is just this once, but I do need to make use of your, er, special talents.' DuVay now had his charm control turned up to 11 even though he knew Wally would see right through it.

'Eeh by 'eck, you don't need to flannel me Henri – I'm a Yorkshireman so just come out with it lad. If I can do it, I will.'

Henri swallowed hard and took a deep breath – he knew that Wally would extract a significant price for what he was about to ask. But that was a conversation for another day. Right now, Henri's main aim was to throw Nursey Corners off the scent so his sneaky plan would work. With Lottie's discovery of the muddy footprints, he knew that Nursey would be investigating. If she was left alone to follow the clues, DuVay was worried that Nursey could ruin everything. Henri resolved he could not let that happen.

'Wally, this is top secret and you will be rewarded accordingly – once, and only once, everything is completed to my entire satisfaction.' Henri tried to inject sufficient menace in his voice to keep Wally on edge.

'Now then Henri, no need to be like that lad – I said I would do it if possible; if not, I won't. And you can rely on my utmost discretion at all times. Confidential is my middle name.'

If only that were actually true thought Henri, as he knew that Wally leaked like an old bucket. But with the time pressures and the Director on his neck, he had no choice. He had to trust Wally.

'OK Wally, so here is the deal. You remember your visit to the Ministry of Sleep?'

'Of course,' confirmed Wally.

'I need you to make someone there disappear.' Henri said this like it was as easy as ordering a take-away pizza.

Wally spluttered and coughed as if he had tried to swallow a particularly large and unpleasant piece of rotten fish.

'Now hold on a minute Henri lad – I'm not a magician and I am most definitely not a murderer. What do you mean by *disappear*?'

'Not permanently of course, just long enough for me to make some, ahem, adjustments to one of the, er, bits of equipment you installed.' Henri was trying not to tell Wally too much. As long as Wally thought he could get away with it that was all that was needed.

'So, who is this person who needs to, as you so delicately put it, disappear? And for how long? And when do they reappear?'

DuVay pondered for a moment. He wasn't sure if he should tell Wally on the phone, or in person. It was probably best he arranged to meet him in person but that would mean travelling to England the next day. Still, that was a small price to pay to ensure that his instructions were clear and that Wally was aware of the consequences of not following them.

'We need to meet in person Wally. You never know who might be listening. I will be at your office tomorrow, 3pm sharp. Be there.'

There was a rustling of what sounded like pages in a book. Henri remembered that Wally had not yet succumbed to having a smartphone and still used a paper diary.

'Right then Henri, that will be OK. See you then. *A bientôt.*' Wally was pleased with himself for recalling that simple French phrase but Henri silently groaned at his awful pronunciation.

.o◯o.

Meanwhile, Felicity had arrived at the Ministry. To avoid any suspicion that she was connected with Nursey, Brad and Angelina had agreed that she would arrive by taxi as if coming from the local station. Brad had taken her to the small branch line station that was the only one to serve that part of the Cotswolds. He ensured she was safely installed and the driver paid in advance.

'Now, remember what Auntie Ange told you Felicity' chided Brad as he hugged her before opening the back door of the Toyota. 'She is Nursey Corners and you don't know her. You have to blend in with others who will be arriving today and not stand out in any way. A good detective never draws attention to themselves, especially when you're working under cover. And if there is ANY problem, you call me first – OK?'

'Yes Dad, you know I will. I'll be OK, promise. I won't let you or auntie – sorry Nursey – down.' She looked at him with her most angelic smile, which was almost completely restored now with the arrival of her adult teeth.

Brad looked at her and nodded. 'I know you will precious. But you can't stop me from worrying. I'm your dad. That's what we dads do – worry about our little girls.'

'I'm not a little girl any more you know – I'm a detective now,' she replied looking very pleased with herself.

Brad suppressed a smile and a tear – he was so proud of her but he knew she hated him telling her.

'Right then Detective Inspector Frampton,' he said with mock formality, 'off you go and solve the case. I expect your report on my desk in the morning.'

Felicity stood to attention and gave him a salute. 'Yes SIR.' She grinned back at him and climbed into the car, pushing her backpack on to the seat ahead of her. And with that the taxi sped off and headed up the hill away from the station.

Brad stood there until it had turned the curve out of view. Now reality arrived and he knew he would not see his daughter for a few more days. But he also knew that his sister would be watching her closely and would be giving him updates. Deep down he knew it was really just a bit of fun but there was a nagging feeling that somehow there was something bigger and a touch odd behind this whole situation. For now, his main responsibility was to Dougie who he had left with his fantastic neighbours and their son of the same age. Dougie was a bit grumpy that he wasn't part of the adventure so he decided to try and find something for him to do that would make him feel involved and useful.

Little did he know that something would come rather sooner than he expected and from a very different source.

Chapter 4

Felicity's taxi stopped at the main gates to the Ministry. They were certainly impressive. Large and ornate black wrought iron gates about 4 metres tall suspended between two massive stone columns topped with carved stone spheres. The driver pressed an intercom and after confirming Felicity's name the gates swung open silently and they proceeded along a wide gravel covered road that led through open parkland dotted with oak trees. The protective fences surrounding their ample trunks spoke of deer and other animals who would have eaten the young shoots.

'Wow this is a lovely place,' Felicity exclaimed as she looked right and left. 'Who owns it?' she asked the driver.

He glanced at her in his mirror. He wasn't used to being quizzed by nine-year-old girls.

'Today it's owned by a medical insurance company in America but it wasn't always. A long time ago it was the family home of Joshua Turner who was a very rich man in these parts. And then it was used as an hospital for injured soldiers. Once the war was over the Turner family sold it to the Americans for a good price as long as they kept the family name alive. People still calls it the Ministry even though it is the Joshua Turner Institute.'

'Gosh, I never knew that,' said Felicity.

'Most people don't, young miss. But he's been a major feature roun' these parts for couple of hunnerd years and provided good employment for local people.' The taxi driver's country burr told her he was also a local man. Felicity had a very well attuned ear for accents as her father had taught her how to differentiate between people from all over the country.

'So, what are you doing here then?' he asked. This was Felicity's first test – she had agreed a cover story with Nursey in case this came up.

'My dad wants to send me to boarding school but he can't until I stop sleep walking. So he thought he would try this place to see if it works.' The words sounded hollow to her as she knew her dad would never send her away but they seemed to convince the taxi driver.

The taxi approached the main building around a large central lawn which led to a massive entrance porch, also in the same honey coloured stone she had seen everywhere on the way from the station. The crunch of the tyres on the gravel was loud in the still summer air. The car stopped at the foot of the steps leading up to an enormous double oak door with sturdy studded black hinges and a door knocker as big as Felicity's arm. She climbed out, her mouth gaping at the size of the house and how lovely it looked against the back drop of its well-tended gardens. Beyond the low wall that marked the edge of the driveway, the ground fell away to reveal a large ornamental pond before the eye was drawn to the far horizon. She dragged her backpack out and turned to see Nursey Corners striding purposefully down the steps to meet her.

'It's Ok, I will be fine now,' she said to the driver who was lingering in the hope of a tip from Nursey. The look on her face quickly convinced him that his luck was out today so he got back in his car and headed down the main driveway to the exit.

'Welcome Miss Frampton,' said Nursey, 'or may I call you Felicity? I am Nursey Corners and I am in charge of the sleep walking programme here at the Joshua Turner Institute - but we just call it the Ministry.'

Felicity nodded. 'The taxi driver told me all about it.'

'Excellent. Good to hear it. And you may call me Nursey – everyone does.' This was all clearly for the benefit of anyone within earshot as Nursey also gave her a huge wink and her biggest smile.

'Thankyou Nursey. Felicity is fine by me,' her niece replied, again somewhat theatrically for the benefit of unseen onlookers. It was best she got into her role from the start as it would help her keep her guard up throughout her stay.

'Jolly good show then – just follow me and I will show you to your quarters. It's all dormitories here so you will be in with the other girls. Not too many at the moment so you will have a choice of beds.' Nursey had switched from being her friendly and fun auntie, to the rather starchy and strict ex-Army nurse that everyone was a little bit scared of.

Off they went, Felicity almost running to keep up with Nursey's long fast stride down the main corridor from which other corridors led to the various dormitories, dining rooms and vast recreational rooms which looked out over the extensive gardens. Another sharp right turn led them to a row of rather substantial looking oak doors sitting inside thick walls. Nursey opened the last one and beckoned to Felicity, who was now about 5 metres behind, to follow her.

Nursey closed the door behind them and waited for Felicity to take in her surroundings. This was Nursey's office and although it was sparsely furnished with just a large leather topped wooden desk, some book cases stuffed with old books and a couple of worn but cosy leather armchairs facing the desk, it was much bigger than any room at Felicity's house. The feeling of space was enhanced by the tall ceilings covered in delicate plaster ornaments and the full-length windows which revealed the most amazing view over the parkland she had just been driven through.

'Nice, isn't it?' asked Nursey. 'This is my office so inside here we can talk more freely but we have to be careful in case anyone comes in. They don't always knock.'

'Wowsers, Auntie Ange this is amazing. You are lucky to have this.' Felicity was still taking it all in, slowly turning through 360 degrees and craning her neck to check out the stucco work.

'The harder I work, the luckier I get,' smiled Nursey. 'Now, one last thing before I show you around and make some introductions. You've got the extra phone we agreed you could keep for emergencies?'

Felicity nodded quickly but also felt in the pocket of her backpack to check it was still there.

'You MUST keep it switched off unless you really need to use it. No-one else will be allowed a phone. When we get to the dorm I will ask you for yours so you can hand me the one I gave you at home, then it looks like you have complied. And if you find anything, just text me the code word we agreed and we can arrange a de-brief – it will probably be in here to avoid too many prying eyes and ears.' Nursey spoke softly and kindly to her niece but once outside her office, her tone would revert to the one she used for her normal dealings with the Ministry.

'Yep, got it – Mum's the word.' Literally – it was quick and easy to send and would not arouse any suspicion if anyone overheard.

'Right, let's show you where you will be staying for the next few days then!' and with that Nursey yanked open the door and strode off with Felicity scrambling to grab her backpack and catch up before Nursey Corners disappeared around a corner.

At what seemed like breakneck speed, Felicity was shown her dorm – only four beds in this one – where her meals would be served, the bathrooms, where she could read books and play with the various games, and all the usual health and safety stuff about fire escapes, fire drills, fire alarms, emergency muster points and so on. Felicity was agog at the vastness of it all and although it was not fitted out with the latest décor it was very cosy and well equipped. The beds looked comfy and were well spaced, with a large bathroom for every four girls so there shouldn't be too many queues for the loos. She had her own wardrobe and bedside table with a nice reading light mounted on the headboard.

The main thing Felicity noticed was the absence of any modern technology. No computers, no Play Stations, no mobile phones, iPads or tablets anywhere. There was a large TV screen in one of the communal rooms but the remote control was hidden. Presumably so that the TV could be turned on and off only by staff. Felicity felt quite comfortable with this as it was similar to how things were at home. Her Dad was pretty strict on watching TV and she was only allowed a basic mobile phone when she went out so she could contact her father, who kept a very close eye on her as he did with Dougie. She had learned how to use the modern smartphone that Nursey had given her so she could hand it over. Felicity had quietly downloaded the special app she used to communicate with her Irish dancing teacher even though she no longer took the lessons. She had decided not to tell Nursey about the app as there was something that Horsey did which normally adults didn't believe. They all thought this was some kind of nick-name but when they found out he was a real horse with some very special talents, their disbelief was always funny to watch. Aside from her Dad, Horsey was the one other individual she could trust completely.

She wondered what the other girls would be like and how they would cope with having their precious iPhones taken away. Most of the girls at her school had them and spent every minute not in class glued to their screens, sending messages to each other and playing games. They thought Felicity was a bit weird for not having one but she didn't care about that. She was more interested in the natural world and she spent her time drawing flowers and trees, as well as identifying all the different plants by their Latin names. Her mind wandered back to the time she had ticked off her Dad for treading on some ants.

'You can't stand on the ants Dad. They have mummies and daddies too,' she had told him, to his considerable surprise and amusement. He soon realised that his daughter thought more deeply about most things than the average gizmo obsessed kid.

She couldn't wait to explore the grounds but she also knew she had to make careful observations for Nursey – and do so without being seen doing it. Her musings were suddenly interrupted by the raucous crackle of a radio and a voice saying, 'The coach is here now Nursey.'

It was Nursey's two-way radio that was on the belt of her uniform.

'Excuse me Felicity. I must go and meet the other new arrivals,' said Nursey with an apologetic look on her face as she knew that from now on she would have to treat her niece just like all the others. She saw Felicity looking at the radio quizzically.

'Oh that? We use them around the grounds and in the house. Much better than mobile phones and a lot cheaper. Bit of a legacy from our military days but it works,' she explained and with that, turned sharply on her heel and strode off towards the entrance.

'Make yourself at home,' she called over her shoulder as she disappeared up the corridor she had brought Felicity down. Felicity watched her disappear and silently chewed her lip for a second, wondering whether to go outside or sit in the big recreation room and wait for the others to be shown around. It was an easy call – the sun was shining and it was a warm afternoon. This might be her only chance to explore the gardens and grounds on her own. She remembered what her father had told her – always get the lie of the land first. You never know when you might need it in a hurry.

How prophetic that advice would soon become.

Chapter 5

It had been an easy drive up from the Channel Tunnel on a Sunday morning and soon enough Henri DuVay was leaving the M40 and heading in the direction of Cheltenham where Wally's offices were located. As Wally had once worked for the main Government department there, he had set up his own business close by when he left the service. It was on a drab industrial estate on the ring road which meant it was cheap and didn't draw attention to itself. All of which suited Wally perfectly given the line of business he was in.

Henri parked in the space marked 'Visitors' and noted that Wally's old 4x4 was also there. Wally came to the door, opened it, glanced around to see if anyone else was lurking nearby and motioned to DuVay to come in quickly. They went through to Wally's office and once the social chit-chat was over and hot drinks had been prepared, Henri sat in the chair opposite Wally's desk and leaned forward.

'As I said Wally we have a problem at the Ministry. The Director suspects that one of his key staff, the woman who runs the sleep walking programme – her name is Nursey Corners - has realised that something is afoot with some foot prints. To be more precise, what she has seen are the footprints left by some of the children we have enticed out of bed. Now, she doesn't know what is going on exactly, but it is only a matter of time before she works it out.' Henri paused to take another sip of his coffee.

'That's grand Henri but where do I come in then? You said it would need special skills,' asked Wally even though he had a pretty good idea of what was going to be expected of him.

'I know this individual Wally. She is very persistent and she is smart. She was the one behind our last deal collapsing so we cannot afford to under-estimate her. We also cannot do anything that involves the Director directly. He must stay above suspicion so we can complete the tests and get the approvals we need to land this contract soon.'

Wally pondered for a moment, stroking his chin slowly.

'OK Henri, so do you have a plan in mind? Or do you want me to work one out? he asked.

'Tell me if you think this will work Wally as it will be you doing it and you will be the one who gets caught if it fails.' Henri wanted to make sure that Wally accepted that the risk was going to be his and that DuVay would not rescue him if things went wrong.

'Somehow, you entice Nursey Corners out after nightfall, get her into one of the caravans, lock the door behind her and drive it off before anyone notices she has gone. You then take it to somewhere that no-one would think of looking and keep her there until we have the approvals from the Director.'

'Well, that is certainly daring Henri, but it is possible. My question is this lad, how do we get her to come outside in the dark? Without arousing suspicions with her or anyone else?'

'Not WE Wally, YOU!' emphasised Henri again.

Wally looked directly at Henri with his eyebrows raised. Henri pondered for a moment as Wally had been rather more perceptive than normal even without saying a word. This was not a trivial question as Henri knew that Nursey was trained to be suspicious of most things after years dealing with Army cadets. He returned Wally's stare without blinking.

'OK Henri, I'll do it. I know a place we can keep her out of sight for a few days where no-one will think of looking. I have a very reliable driver who is used to not being noticed. And I think I have a way to ensure she comes outside. She may be suspicious by nature but she is also curious. Leave it with me,' said Wally looking rather pleased with himself.

'When will you be able to start Wally?' asked DuVay, 'We don't have much time. Soon the Ministry will be empty as school holidays are almost over and the Director is getting very impatient.'

'Leave it with me Henri. I will speak to my team and we should be able to put the plan into action within a couple of days – absolute maximum,' Wally assured him with a firm handshake.

'D'accord, merci' Henri momentarily lapsed into French as he knew even Wally understood those two words.

'I will also update the Director later this evening,' said Henri and turned to leave.

He paused briefly at the door and looked at Wally to try and see if there was any sign of concern or him being unsure. Wally beamed a smile back at him as if to say, *'trust me, it will be fine.'*

'You know where to reach me Henri if you have any concerns,' added Wally as if he had read the Frenchman's mind. And with that Henri jumped into his car – he was off to make his dinner engagement with the Director.

When the Frenchman had roared off in his car, Wally slumped back in his comfy old chair and put his feet up on his desk.

'Bloomin' Ada, how am I going to get that woman into me car without her putting up a fight?' he mused to himself. Whatever else Wally was, violence was not part of his make- up. He had always been brought up by his farmer father to treat ladies with courtesy and respect. A lopsided smile crept over his thin lips.

`Oh well, I'll just 'ave to use me natural charm then' he said out loud, looking at his reflection in the office window. Sadly, the receding hairline and prominent nose looking back at him didn't quite support his assessment.

.oOo.

At the Ministry, the Director had other matters to deal with before his forthcoming meeting with Henri. He wasn't really looking forward to it as he knew that trying to get the elusive Frenchman to do what he wanted was always tricky.

For now, however, he was getting ready to speak to the new arrivals at the Ministry in this the last week of the school holidays. Normally the children who arrived at this time were not very happy at giving up their final few days of freedom and so it was always a challenge to get them settled in and doing things the way they should be. Even though he had accepted what was supposed to be a gentle and easy position, Bertie was still nervous. He actually disliked children intensely. He had never had his own family – too busy with the Army – and simply didn't understand the behaviour of the kids in his charge. This led him to appear awkward and a little creepy to children at times, so they tended to keep their distance from him. But this was something he just had to do and his aim was to get it over and done as quickly as possible.

As Nursey Corners directed them into the main recreation room her eyes were also on Felicity. Her niece was not usually the most sociable child and tended to hang back until she had sussed out the others and decided who she would talk to first. But once she saw that Felicity was already speaking to several of the other new guests she was able to relax and focus on her own role for the next 20 minutes or so.

Nursey rang her little bell which was a relic from the days when the building had servants to attend to the owners' every need. But its gentle tinkling had the desired effect and the forty or so children stopped their excited babble and looked towards the tall, imposing figure of the Director in his country style tweed suit, brightly coloured waistcoat and dark brown brogues.

'Ahemmrummpf,' spluttered the Director as he cleared his throat to speak but also to get their attention.

'Good afternoon girls and boys, my lords, ladies and gentlemen.' This always raised a titter around the room and today was no exception, 'Und Wilkommen,' he added for good measure as he knew there was one German boy but wisely decided not to test his language abilities any further.

'Welcome to the Joshua Turner Memorial Institute for Advanced Research into Sleep Problems in Children, or as we are usually known because it is much easier to say, the "Ministry of Sleep".' Again, the Director waited for the usual chuckle.

'I am Director Bedstead and I am in charge of this er, um, magnificent establishment and I am sure you are all familiar now with its layout. Helping me with the various, er, treatments, I have a very experienced and capable staff, led by Nursey Corners whom most of you have now met.' Bertie glanced over to see that Nursey was smiling and nodding to the children to make sure they knew who she was.

`Our job is to help you get a really good night's sleep and our success rate is very high.'

A murmur of *ooh's* and *aah's* crackled around the room.

'However,' he paused a few seconds for what he assumed was dramatic effect, 'we cannot do this without your help. We look to each and every one of you to fully cooperate with your mentors and instructors. Our rules are strict and everyone is expected to uphold them because they are designed to send you home having achieved your objective.'

He looked around to see lots of nodding heads and a few worried looks from those who were clearly not used to having to do what adults told them. He sensed this would be a difficult week but pressed on with the rest of his well-worn speech. Finally, it came to an end.

'And now boys and girls, please make your way through to the dining room where supper will be served. Enjoy your stay at the Ministry and don't hesitate to let us know if you need help, or have any questions or concerns.'

Nursey Corners thought to herself, *'Yeah, right, like you will be the one getting up in the middle of the night to change the sheets if someone has a little accident.'*

The Director looked around the room and beamed his best and biggest smile to them all, turned on his heel and marched swiftly out of the room and towards his private quarters with a quiet sigh of relief.

As the children started to move towards the dining room, Nursey noticed that Felicity was in earnest conversation with the German boy.

She remembered his name was Wilhelm which he had pronounced in a perfect English accent.

'What have you come to the Ministry for Wilhelm?' asked Felicity, reading his name badge. 'I'm here for sleep walking as my dad wants me to go to boarding school next year.' She thought that by telling him about herself he would also tell her more about himself.

'Please, call me Will,' he said, 'it is easier to remember.'

'Of course, Will. Are you German – you sound, er, very English?' Felicity looked at him quizzically.

'I am German yes, but I was born in the UK and I go to school here. My mum and dad are German and my dad came over here with his job before I was born. But we go back to Germany a lot to see my grandparents who live in the Black Forest.' Her tactic seemed to be working as he was talking quite freely about himself, so she decided to push her luck.

'Wow that sounds interesting. I've never been to Germany. I'd love to go sometime. It looks very pretty in the pictures I've seen,' enthused Felicity. 'So, what programme are you on at the Ministry?' Will looked a little embarrassed and blushed slightly without making eye contact.

'I have a weak bladder,' he said, 'and sometimes, I don't make it to the toilet in time. My papa says I have to learn to control it otherwise I will not be able to go on holiday with them. So they have sent me here where no-one will know me.'

'Oh, that's a bit unfair,' Felicity consoled him. 'I mean, being sent away to where no-one knows you.'

'But you have been sent here too – do you know anyone here?' he countered gently.

Felicity had to bite her tongue to avoid blurting out that actually her aunt basically ran the place and just smiled. 'But I know you now and we can be friends, can't we?' she said brightly.

'OK Felicity,' replied Will leaning forward to check her name on her badge as he had forgotten it already.

They walked into the dining room to find that they had all been assigned places at various tables. This was to ensure that everyone mixed and avoided the formation of little cliques which usually meant the shy ones were left alone and felt excluded. Nursey Corners was well aware of how children could behave at this age and for her methods to work effectively, it was vital that no-one was allowed to suffer in solitude. After all they would soon be sharing dormitories.

Felicity quickly found her two room-mates for the week, Gail and Amanda, sitting at the same table as her along with a few other girls on the sleep walking programme. They looked to be about her age so she felt comfortable. Felicity didn't mind mixing with older girls but she had found that they often looked down on those younger and didn't share as much as they should.

Amanda looked quite posh to Felicity. Her clothes were all new and didn't look as if they came from chain stores judging by the up-market logos on them. She had thick lustrous hair down to her shoulders, lovely skin and long elegant fingers like a pianist.

When Felicity had spoken to her and called her Amanda, she had just said, 'Everyone calls me Mandy. You can too if you like. Only my mother calls me Amanda and usually only when she is bossing me around. Which is *all the time!*' Mandy laughed and rolled her eyes as she said this. Gail and Felicity gave a little chuckle.

She didn't sound at all posh – just normal, so Felicity let out a silent sigh as she had been worried that Amanda would not really speak to her. It just reminded her what her own mother had always told her, *'don't judge a book by its cover – most people are nice if you are nice to them.'*

Gail was completely different. She was very giggly and talked at a furious rate in a lilting Scottish accent, her curly red hair swishing from side to side like a horse's tail swatting flies. She had freckles and her front teeth were still emerging which meant she sometimes whistled her 'S' when she spoke.

`Ah've never been tae England before,' she gabbled breathlessly. 'It's FAB. Everyone is so nice, so they are. Ah mean, people are nice in Scotland too but they all think the English are a bit stuck up. Ah dinnae. Ah think it's BRILLIANT here!' Gail almost bounced in her seat as she spoke.

Dinner arrived, served by two young girls wearing aprons, who were from the local village. They were used to seeing a huge range of children and were under strict instructions from Nursey not to speak too much as she didn't want them distracted by stories of the outside world. By this time the kids were hungry and wolfed down the fresh penne pasta with home-made Bolognese sauce (although there was a cheese sauce option if anyone didn't eat meat).

Puddings followed. The food would become more *'healthy'* tomorrow but on their first night away from home, Nursey just wanted to give them something they would all eat and that wasn't too challenging for anyone with delicate tastes.

As the dishes were cleared away, Felicity glanced out of the window and spotted the Director furtively looking around him before getting into his car and driving off down the same gravel approach she had come up only a few hours ago. She didn't know if this was normal or not, but now that she was in full detective mode, she made a mental note of it and would inform Nursey when they had their first debrief. But before then, she had a night to get through in a shared room with two known sleep walkers. The adventure, as she saw it to be, was about to start in earnest.

Chapter 6

The warmth of the late summer evening started to relent and a refreshing coolness settled over the grounds of the Ministry. Birds started making their way back to their nests and roosting sites, calling and cawing to their friends as they did. As the sun dipped below the horizon, the shadows from the trees crept ever closer to the main house.

Felicity loved this time of evening normally. She and Dougie would often be outside in the back garden. They would be playing the games they'd invented during the day whilst their dad sat on the patio with a glass of his favourite wine. He usually watched them out of the corner of his eye with a contented smile. Although that could have just been the wine. But tonight, Felicity was focused on the task she had been asked to perform by her aunt, Nursey Corners. She was weighing up the possibilities. Should she pretend to fall asleep with the other girls in her dorm, or somehow stay awake and observe what went on? Given that she had no idea what to expect, the only thing to do, she said to herself was, *'observe, note and maintain silence,'* as per the instructions her dad had given her just before they left the house. First and foremost, she had to establish a routine with Mandy and Gail that would not appear odd to them, so if anything out of the ordinary *did* happen, she would spot it at once.

'Which bed would you like?' she addressed both of her room-mates.

'Ah'd like the one by the window,' chirped Gail, before anyone had a chance to stake a better claim.

Felicity and Mandy glanced at each other as if to say, *'OK with me,'* as neither of them really wanted to be by a large open window.

'Can I have the one by the door to the bathroom?' asked Mandy. 'Just in case I need to get up in the night, I don't want to disturb anyone.'

Felicity looked at Gail for any sign this was a problem. It wasn't.

'OK for me Mandy,' said Felicity, 'I'll take the one nearest the other door then.' She was secretly hoping that would be the case as it meant she could see anything that involved the other girls leaving the room in the night.

With that, they set about unpacking their bags and putting things away in their wardrobes and dressers. Each bed was identical with identical sheets, pillows and blankets, as were the other facilities for each of them, so there was no difference, just one of personal preference depending on what they were used to at home.

The bathroom had two separated areas each with a bath, loo, basin and a shower cubicle. It was all pretty basic - not what you'd call luxurious - but it worked and gave them sufficient privacy for their needs. The Ministry had once been a private home but when it was acquired by the Government and transformed into what it was today, the budget was modest and it wasn't possible to give each person individual treatment. So, this was a half-way house really, but it had worked for most who came into the Ministry. Once or twice Nursey had to deal with a few sensitive souls not used to sharing and who found the whole experience somewhat traumatic.

Felicity let Gail and Mandy go first and brush their teeth, comb their hair and do the essentials before going to bed. Nursey was very clear that lights out came at 9pm so they were all anxious to be in bed by then.

As Felicity got into her pyjamas and started to peel back the sheet and blanket that had been tucked around her bed like a shrink-wrapped sausage, she heard Nursey's voice in the next dorm. A few seconds later Nursey appeared in the doorway.

'Good evening girls – Mandy, Gail and, um, Felicity.' She feigned not being able to remember her niece's name.

'Good evening Nursey,' they all chorused, but not feeling quite as confident as they sounded.

'Now, just to remind you of a few rules we have here at the Ministry. These are all for your own good as we know they work.' She looked at each girl in turn to ensure they had accepted her authority. They had.

'First, there is no chit chat after lights out. You are to do your best to get to sleep. After all that's why you're here – to help overcome a little problem. Isn't that right?' Again, Nursey looked around for nodding heads.

'Secondly, if you need to use the bathroom in the night, please try to avoid turning on the main lights in the dorm. Only turn on the bathroom light once you are inside and the door is closed. To that end I do suggest you familiarise yourself with the layout and where the light switches are.'

'Thirdly, we have developed a special approach here at the Ministry to help you with your problem. You will have seen the small speakers above your bed?' She looked at each girl – they all automatically looked up.

'You will hear some nice soothing music and natural sounds from them but they will be very quiet and only last until you are asleep. We've done extensive research and we know this helps you get a full night's rest.' No-one commented – which was the normal response.

'Finally, I know you are all a little nervous being away from home.' Nursey paused to look at each girl in turn, this time radiating sympathy and kindness. 'So, if you do wake up and feel a little, shall we say, homesick, then by each bed is a small red button. If you press it, the night nurse, Lottie, will come and see what the problem is. This is not a prison, or even a hospital, it's a place where we want to help you.' Nursey fervently hoped that this was in line with what their parents had told them but she knew from past experience that some of the less enlightened ones saw the Ministry as a way to instil in their children the confidence they had failed to inspire. She inspected each bed in turn to make sure her signature, *'Nursey Corners,'* remained in place.

'Thankyou Nursey.' Felicity spoke first. 'I think we'll be OK.'

'Yes Nursey, we're OK,' both Mandy and Gail said at the same time and then giggled that they had said the same thing together. They looked at each other and Felicity – they were all on the same page.

'OK you three that's just what I want to hear.' Nursey smiled and turned to leave, looking over her shoulder one last time and making eye contact with each in turn, but lingering a fraction longer with Felicity. She wanted to be able to call her brother and update him with good news – that his beloved daughter was OK and settled in safely.

The darkness that followed Nursey turning out the lights was much deeper than most of them were used to. There was very little light pollution at the Ministry so there was no need for curtains to maintain the atmosphere in the room.

And so, they were all able to drift off into a deep untroubled sleep, including Felicity who was pretty tired from all her travels and efforts of the past few days. Silence descended, stillness pervaded every part of the Ministry, except the garden where the faint screeching of owls could be heard in the far distance.

Lottie peeked into Felicity's dorm before she went back to the 'Light Bulb' section where those who needed a night light were also fast asleep with just a faint glow compared to the almost complete darkness of the sleep walking section. She turned down the night lights to their minimum level once she had established that everyone was sleeping and flicked on the switch for the monitoring system for the sleep walkers so she could keep an eye on everyone without leaving her desk. Before too long, Lottie's head dropped as she sat in her swivel chair with her feet on the desk, her eyes heavy with sleep and she too nodded off. All was silent – well, apart from the regular snorts and grunts from the snorers' group but they were oblivious to the noise they made, just as Lottie now was.

.oOo.

The Director's dinner with Henri was at the coffee stage in the upmarket hotel dining room that was his preferred location for discrete discussions. The staff knew him well and kept a respectful distance when not bringing food or topping up wine glasses.

'So, we're agreed then Henri?' said the Director fixing the Frenchman with a steely gaze over his half-moon spectacles.

Henri nodded gently before responding. 'Yes Director, we are. I will take care of your little problem with the nurse so that she won't be able to blow our cover, if you will pardon the pun,' confirmed Henri, smirking at his own joke.

'Once she is out of the way, you will sign the approvals for the contract and send it to the commercial guys. Then the orders will arrive and we'll both be rich.'

'Indeed we will Henri, but I must remind you how important it is that we do not have a repeat of the mistakes made last time. You know there is a great focus on buying British made goods so having labels saying, *'Made in France'* only creates problems and people asking too many questions.' The Director's tone was gentle but his words were spoken in a way that left Henri in no doubt this was his last chance.

'So, one last time – you will have the caravan waiting in the place we discussed out of sight of the security cameras, the music will be the correct version we have uploaded to the system and your driver knows exactly where to take Nursey Corners?' He leaned forward towards Henri, his eyes unblinking. Henri slowly nodded his agreement.

'And she won't be harmed – is that clear too?'

'One hundred percent clear, you have my word.' Henri replied with his most serious face on. He knew that the Director had a bit of a soft spot for Nursey Corners and only wanted her out of the way long enough to allow them to complete their plan. The plan that would make them both comfortably rich in an idyllic Caribbean island. What could possibly go wrong now?

'OK old chap,' said the Director getting to his feet and calling for the bill from the waiter, 'let's keep in touch as required. Secure channels only of course, you know the drill.' Henri too stood up and shook the Director's hand warmly.

'This time next year Bertie, we'll all be millionaires.'

The Director frowned for a moment. He was sure he had heard that line somewhere else but couldn't think quite where.

.oOo.

Back in the darkness of Felicity's dorm, she was awakened by the rustling sound of bed sheets being pushed back, followed by the soft 'plop' of feet on the polished wooden floor. She froze in her bed not wishing to move.

She half opened one eye to see two shadowy figures walk past her and into the dimly lit corridor outside.

Outside, an owl screeched, this time a lot louder and closer than before. She also noticed that the music still seemed to be playing although it didn't sound quite the same. In an instant, she made her mind up what she should do next.

Chapter 7

Felicity was now wide awake and her eyes were growing accustomed to the pitch-black darkness. She waited until the sound of the footsteps from her two room-mates had faded sufficiently so that they would not notice her creeping along behind them. Easing the tightly bound sheets away she slipped her feet into the trainers she had left by the side of her bed and started off towards the exit.

She heard the creak of the door open followed by footsteps on the gravel. Gail and Mandy had gone outside.

Felicity moved quickly and silently to the door and listened. Only footsteps receding.

To her, it felt like her heart was pounding like a bass drum and could be heard everywhere, but she took a couple of deep breaths and calmly slipped through the smallest opening she could manage in the door and into the cool night air.

Scanning the gardens and the path leading to the back of the house she caught a glimpse of Gail and Mandy, in their pyjamas but barefoot, just as they disappeared from view around a large rhododendron bush that bordered the path. Felicity waited for a few seconds so she would not be within earshot of them and then crossed the path on to the grass where she could move silently. The one thing she knew about sleep walkers was that you should not wake them up suddenly whilst they were actually sleep walking. Besides, she was determined to see what they did and try to find out why they were walking in the garden of all places.

She darted quickly forward to where the girls had rounded the curve and paused, using the shadow of the bush to keep her hidden, just in case anyone saw her. She and Dougie had played endless games of hide and seek like this, creeping up on each other only to leap out shouting 'BOO!' to make the other one jump. Little had she realised that one day she would be doing it for real, at night in her pyjamas.

Felicity detected a faint sound coming from about 100 metres away which seemed to be where there was also a dim yellow patch of light. Unless she was very much mistaken, it was coming from the window of a caravan. There was no sign of Gail or Mandy. Everything was dark and silent apart from the as yet unidentified sound. She swallowed hard, wondering where they might have gone. She could just about make out that the gravel path only went one way and did not seem to have any turn off or branches along it, so that must be where they had gone.

But where?

Surely they hadn't just disappeared into the night air? Had they been kidnapped? She tip-toed silently towards the source of the sound and the light, listening intently for anything that might indicate where Gail and Mandy had gone.

With her heart now pounding she knew she had to locate her two friends and help them if they were in trouble, even if it meant taking the risk of waking them up. Felicity ran as quickly and quietly as she could in the direction they had taken. As she rounded the curve in the path, suddenly Gail and Mandy came into view, heading back towards the dorm. Felicity stopped dead in her tracks and looked around. They hadn't spotted her. She had to make an instant decision – stay and confront them? Or run back undetected? In a heartbeat she knew – best not to be seen, so she ran at full tilt back the way she had just come, glancing once over her shoulder to make sure they had not seen her. Felicity arrived back at the dorm breathless. She pulled off her trainers and walked as silently as she could back to the room and quickly got into bed, shoving them underneath and pulling the covers over her head just as she heard the main door close downstairs. She hoped they would not hear her heart pounding as their footsteps got even closer until the door handle on the dorm moved silently downwards.

Felicity held her breath, screwed her eyes tightly shut and prayed they would not realise she was in fact awake.

But she need not have worried. Gail and Mandy went to their own beds and got back in as if nothing had happened.

.oOo.

The next morning, after Gail and Mandy were ready to go to breakfast, Felicity had made an excuse she needed to go to the bathroom and waited for them to leave.

'I'll only be a minute,' she said, 'just need to use the loo.'

She quickly delved into her bedside locker and felt in the inside pocket of her backpack for the phone she had been allowed to keep for exactly this kind of situation. She turned it on, waited for the signal strength indicator to show she had connection and sent the agreed single code word to Nursey. Once she had the 'message sent' response, she deleted the message from the sent folder, turned it off and put it back where she had kept it.

She then went down to breakfast and sat with her friends as if nothing had happened.

'Sorry about that,' said Felicity as she poured some milk on her cereal. 'Did you sleep OK? I was out like a light.' Well it was a bit of a fib, but they were not to know that she had woken up just as quickly when they left the room. 'Oh yes, it was FAB' said Gail, 'I slept like a baby for the first time in weeks. Must have been that music.'

'Me too,' chimed in Mandy, 'I thought it was a bit spooky at first as it was so dark, but once I got used to it, it was fine.'

They seemed totally unaware they had been up and about outside in the night, Felicity thought to herself. She caught Nursey's eye as she walked past and the subtle inclination of Nursey's head towards the door. That was the sign that Nursey had got the coded text message and wanted to speak to Felicity. Felicity got up from the table as if to get more food and caught Nursey's whispered message.

'Come to my office Felicity,' Nursey Corners whispered to her niece. 'We need to find out what is going on quickly.'

'OK, as soon as I can,' mouthed Felicity silently, spooning more cereal into her bowl and picking up a slice of toast as well.

.oOo.

The rest of breakfast seemed to take ages but eventually everyone was finished and started to head off to their various planned activities. Some were playing ball games outside, others were drawing and a few decided to join in the music lessons on various instruments. It all looked like good fun to Felicity but she had other things in mind. Like how to get to Nursey's office undetected and then explain her absence to Gail and Mandy who no doubt would be looking out for her. After a moment's thought and consideration of how big a fib she would have to tell, she decided to go with the *'upset tummy'* routine.

She tapped lightly on the office door, which was slightly ajar, and peeked around the edge of the door to see Nursey at her desk. Nursey walked over quickly, scanned up and down the corridor to make sure there was no-one watching, and nodded to Felicity to come inside.

'Well Felicity, it looks like you've been busy.' Nursey smiled at her both pleased and, inside, a little concerned that she may be letting her niece in for more than she wanted. 'Tell me what happened?'

Felicity recounted how she had followed her room-mates to the point where they seemed to just disappear.

Nursey listened intently, making notes on her pad as the story unfolded.

'So, what did you do then?' Nursey looked up from her writing.

'Well, I stayed close to the big bushes and got closer. I could still see the light and the sound was getting louder. But there was still no sign of Gail or Mandy.' Felicity almost whispered as she recalled how odd it felt to be out there in the garden, in the dark, trying to find two apparently missing girls her own age. Nursey nodded at her to go on and made a note.

'Then I saw it,' said Felicity.

'Saw what?' exclaimed Nursey, her eyebrows almost disappearing under her nurse's head band.

'I'm not quite sure,' continued Felicity, 'I was scared to get too close in case anyone saw me. But it looked like a caravan.'

Nursey looked at Felicity with her jaw dropped open. 'A caravan?'

Felicity nodded. 'Yes, I'm sure that is what it looked like. It was sort of white and had a door.'

'What on earth would a caravan be doing here?' mused Nursey. 'And more to the point, how did it get in?'

'I don't know Auntie Ange, sorry, Nursey. But after about five minutes I heard the door of it open and the music was playing.'

'Can you remember what the music was?' asked Nursey.

'Sort of,' replied Felicity, 'it sounded like the music you said would be playing to get us to sleep. Except it was a bit different – it was more like the music that was playing when Gail and Mandy left the dorm.'

'Different? In what way? We only have one piece of music that I am aware of.' Nursey looked puzzled.

'It had a strange rumbling sound that was a bit like, I know this is really weird, but it was a bit like tap dancing. But not – it seemed a bit more muffled but there was a rhythm to it.'

'That IS odd' Nursey said, her face betraying a frown. 'There is no dancing on the tape. I supervised it myself.'

'And there was something else.' Felicity whispered again. 'I could definitely hear something like singing. I'm not sure what it was as I couldn't make out any words. But it did sound familiar.'

Nursey leaned back in her chair and left out a long slow whistling breath. This was not what she had expected. That music was the crux of her treatment, along with the way the bed sheets were tightly tucked in to make it harder to get out of bed. There was no way it could have dancing and singing on it. She would be taking this up with their technical expert, Kurt.

'What did you do then,' asked Nursey, 'once you had heard this odd music?'

'I ran back to the dorm,' said Felicity, 'I didn't want to be seen. I was pretty sure that was where Gail and Mandy had gone to. When I got back into bed and pretended to be asleep, they both came back a few minutes later and climbed into their beds. I could just about see in the dark. They were still asleep. Which is why they both told me this morning that had slept really well. So they didn't know what they had done.'

Nursey again paused to think about what Felicity had told her and what they should do next. Clearly something was going on. It was too much of a coincidence for two new girls to sleep walk and, apparently, to a caravan with odd music playing. It just didn't make sense. But Nursey knew that the answers were there – all they had to do was find them. The last thing she wanted was to put Felicity in harm's way but without her she would not be able to get all the information that her niece could, and would therefore potentially miss some vital clue.

'You've done incredibly well, Felicity. But we'll need to find out more. For now, just keep your eyes and ears open and let me know if we need to meet again. I will let your dad know you're OK. He'll be very proud of you. As I am too.'

'What are you going to do now then?' asked Felicity.

'Good question young lady. First, I am going to speak to our resident technical expert, Herr Doktor Kurt Noisy-Fridge. Kurt made the recordings to my exact specifications and there is no way I know of that there could be a different one. If there is, Kurt is the man to find out. He is an expert in rumbling noises – or rather, how to eliminate them from noisy fridges. That's how he got his nick-name and it has sort of stuck. But he is a proper engineer.' Nursey used her most authoritative voice to try to convey to Felicity that all was well and they would soon get to the bottom of the strange goings on. She would only involve the Director once she was in possession of the full facts and a way forward.

She did not realise that, rather like the lookout on the Titanic, they had only seen the tip of the iceberg. With that she let Felicity go and re-join her friends. Appearances had to be maintained at all times.

Chapter 8

Sure enough, their curiosity got the better of them. As soon as Felicity returned to the main groups, Gail and Mandy came over to her.

'We missed you – where have you been? We thought you'd want to play some games?' said Gail, looking a little sad. She seemed to have taken quite a shine to Felicity.

'Yeah, me too – can you play with us now?' asked Mandy.

'I had to see the nurse – I've got a bit of an upset tummy. Probably something I had on holiday before I came here,' said Felicity, trying to look apologetic and a little ill at the same time. Given she was normally extremely healthy and rarely had colds or the bugs that other kids of her age came down with, this was proving a little tricky.

'Oh dear, that's not good news. Hope you're OK?' Gail looked more sympathetic now, as did Mandy.

'Sure, I'm OK. Just got a pill to take. It will be fine,' Felicity reassured them. 'Now, what are we going to play?' And with that the three new friends found a suitable board game and a table, passing the next few hours absorbed in the game and learning a bit more about each other. Felicity was happy to forget being a sleuth and enjoyed being able to play with other girls her own age without having to worry too much about a younger brother who only wanted to play football.

.oOo.

'Kurt? It's Nursey Corners here. We need to talk.' Nursey barked down the phone at the hapless Kurt. He was well used to her methods and mannerisms but he still bristled when she was a little too, how would he put it, officious? He knew she had a long career in the Army behind her and that old soldiering habits were hard to change, but he just wished sometimes that she would speak to him normally rather than every exchange feeling like a set of orders or a cross examination.

'Good morning to you too Nursey,' replied Kurt, ignoring the urgency in her voice. 'How can I help you today?

What seems to be the problem?'

'Can't talk on the phone Kurt. We need to meet. Are you free now?' Nursey was not relenting on the barking.

'Let me check my diary Nursey ... hold the line please.' Kurt put his hand over the mouthpiece of his phone and swore out loud. He knew he was free but he didn't want to just agree on the spot.

'I have something to finish now,' he said, looking at the cup of coffee he had just made from his shiny new personal machine that he didn't want to share with anyone, 'but if you give me 15 minutes, you can come over to my office then.'

Nursey looked at the watch on her apron – upside down to others of course, which meant it could be read by her easily. '10.45 hours it is then,' and she hung up without another word.

Kurt sighed and tried not to let her approach get to him. He knew she was a kind and caring nurse so he did his best to overlook how she made him feel like a naughty cadet at times.

.oOo.

Two sharp raps on his door told him it was Nursey – and looking at the clock on his wall, the minute hand clicked into place at precisely 10.45. At least he could rely on Nursey to be on time.

'Do come in Nursey,' he called.

She sat down on his guest chair without waiting to be asked. His office was rather more than just an office. It was also his workshop where all the electronic and technical stuff lived. The things that kept the Ministry secure, connected and well managed. In an air-conditioned room, next to where he sat, behind smoked glass panels, were a couple of racks of black boxes all with lights flashing, some green, a few red and others plain white. There were more cables than anyone could count.

'Kurt, I need your help,' began Nursey. 'You know the recording we made for the sleep walking programme? The one with the soothing music and the sounds of waves and stuff?'

'Of course I know it – I put it on the system,' confirmed Kurt, bristling a little at being asked such basic information.

'This may sound a little strange. Well, very strange actually. I can't tell you how I know this … but first … I need you to promise me this conversation goes no further.'

'You have my word,' Kurt said holding her gaze and starting to feel slightly nervous inside.

'There is another recording. One that sounds a lot like the one we made, but is different. And it is being played in the dorms.' Nursey looked at him to see how he would react. Kurt blew slowly through his pursed lips and tried to stay calm. What Nursey was saying was of course impossible as only he had access to the system so either she was hearing things that didn't exist, or she was saying he had screwed up somehow. For now, Kurt suspended belief and told himself that

Nursey would not be making wild accusations about him, so there was more to this.

'I'm not aware of any recording but yours Nursey. But if you say there is a different one then of course we must investigate. Let me check now – it will take about 10 minutes for me to do a thorough scan of the main system we used to store your music. Do you want to wait or come back?'

'I'll wait,' said Nursey, 'but maybe you could make me a nice cup of coffee from that fancy new machine you have?' She smiled at him – she knew of course that he had it and that he thought no-one else knew he did. Finally, she had got one over on him. Her competitive streak was intact and well.

'Of course,' said Kurt, cursing himself for leaving it out on display and putting a new capsule in it. He unlocked his desk drawer and took out the swipe card that allowed him access to the equipment room. He could have done it from the terminal on his desk of course, but he didn't want Nursey to see what he did just in case there really was something.

Kurt swiped the card in the reader and entered the code into the key pad by the door. The door clicked open and he went in. Nursey sat and sipped the excellent coffee and gazed around Kurt's office. It was quite bare from a creature comforts point of view. Just a large desk, some trays of documents, an extension phone for the Ministry system and a pin-board with various things stuck to it. Nursey got up to take a look. Nothing abnormal, just a few yellow sticky notes with what looked like phone numbers, an article from a computer journal and some business cards for taxi firms, take away food and the like. One caught her eye – WSB Technical Services with a Cheltenham address. Obviously not food then. She had never heard of WSB but they were probably an electrical firm of some kind. Nursey sat back down in her chair and looked into the air-conditioned room. Kurt was hunched over the screen and looking a little worried.

He came back through the open the door and it clicked shut behind him with a solid "thunk" and a hiss of cold air escaping. He was clutching a printed sheet of what looked to Nursey like a lot of gobbledegook technical stuff she didn't understand. Kurt's face had gone pale – a whiter shade of pale in fact. He was shaking his head gently and tugging at his ear lobe.

'This is impossible,' he started, 'but it has happened.'

'What has happened Kurt? Nursey pressed him looking as concerned as Kurt felt.

'You're right. There IS a second recording on the system. I have no idea how it got there or who put it there.' Kurt looked up at Nursey with complete confusion on his face.

'This is serious Kurt. It means there has been a security breach. Which means we will HAVE to tell the Director.' Nursey was fully aware of what this meant and was as aghast as Kurt.

'Not yet Nursey. If we tell him and we don't know how it happened, well, you know what he's like. He will go, how do you say, bonkers?'

'So how do we find out then Kurt?' Nursey was asking as much for information as she was in order to put pressure on him to do the finding out. 'Can you let me have a copy of the other version so I can listen to it? Maybe that will give us a clue?'

Deep down Nursey knew that she didn't really have a clue. She resolved to ask Felicity – after all, that was why she had asked her niece to help her. And it was Felicity who had spotted the difference so if anyone might know, it would be her.

'Yes of course. I'll make you a CD now,' Kurt offered.

'No, not a CD. Anyone could find that. Put it on my iPhone and then I can password protect it,' instructed Nursey, getting her phone out and unlocking it.

'You're right. I should have thought of that. Sorry Nursey. It's been a real shock. I will get to the bottom of it.'

'Thankyou Kurt – I'm not blaming you,' Nursey assured him, although she was not sure why. After all, he was the only one who had the right passwords to access the system so if not him, then who was it? And how?

Kurt made the copy for the iPhone and handed it back to Nursey.

'Let me listen to this privately,' she said, 'if someone has put it there, it is there for a reason. And the reason may be in what is different. After all, why do it if it isn't different?' Nursey was not sure she knew the answers to any of those questions or if they were even the right questions, but she did know that her niece was the best person to find out why. She would see or hear things without an adult's cluttered mindset. Children often saw things in much simpler and clearer terms than adults.

Time was marching on and with the revelations about the possible caravan that was also mysteriously in the Ministry grounds at night, it was obvious there was a connection. This was simply too much of a coincidence. They had to find the link. And they had to do it without whoever was behind this realising they knew, otherwise they might never find out. Absolute secrecy was essential. But now there were three people involved. Felicity she could trust of course but she could not control who else might see something as well. Kurt would not say anything as he would be too embarrassed to admit that his security systems had been breached. There was no choice – she had to carry on and stay vigilant. But before that Felicity had to hear what was on the phone.

Chapter 9

Felicity was totally engrossed in her game with the other girls, Mandy and Gail. She didn't notice Nursey Corners approaching her from behind until she felt her warm, gentle hand on her shoulder. She turned around with a start to see her aunt smiling at her.

'Sorry to startle you Felicity,' began Nursey, 'but I just need you to sign your consent for the tablets I provided this morning for your upset tummy.' Nursey was in full-on, professional nurse mode now and there was no way that Felicity's room-mates would have suspected anything else. They had agreed on the cover story as it allowed them to use it when needed so Felicity could make a recovery or her '*condition*' could get worse, depending on how often she and Nursey needed to confer. Better to do it openly than try to hide it as that always resulted in somebody finding out.

'Of course, Nursey,' replied Felicity.

'Could you just pop through to my office when you are finished and we can take care of it. I will need to send a copy to your father as well.' Felicity recognised the coded message that her aunt was delivering and nodded her agreement.

'We're almost done,' said Gail, 'looks like you've won.'

'Yeah, thought you said you hadn't played this before,' Mandy added, realising that they had been well beaten.

'Beginners' luck,' retorted Felicity. 'I'll just go and see what Nursey wants and then we can have some lunch. I'm starving ...'

'Thought you had a dicky tummy? Gail asked her with a twinkle in her eye. Felicity decided not to comment and just left them with a *'see you soon'* over her shoulder as she went off to find Nursey. She sat down in her office and looked at Nursey expectantly.

'You were right Felicity,' her aunt confirmed looking very proud of her niece, 'there WAS a second version of our sleeping music but no-one knew it was there. We have very tight security as you know but somehow this got in. Kurt is working on it as he is completely baffled. And more than a little bit embarrassed. As am I. So, we have agreed to let you listen to the recording, as you spotted it, to see if there is anything we can detect that might tell us why anyone would do such a thing. If we know why, we might work out how.'

'Wow, that's amazing,' cooed Felicity, secretly chuffed that she had found something real. 'Ok, let me take a listen – where is it?'

'It's on my phone – I had Kurt make a copy. You ready? I'll just play it as it is.' With that Nursey tapped her phone and left it on the desk where they could both hear it. Felicity listened carefully as she wasn't too familiar yet with the original version. The recording lasted about two minutes and Nursey stopped it.

'Well, what do you think?' asked Nursey.

'That's definitely the one I heard in the dorm as Mandy and Gail started sleep walking,' confirmed Felicity. 'And it is the same one I heard in the garden.'

'Excellent – now what do you think is different?'

'Hmmm … hard to say exactly, but what I can hear for sure is that there is a definite rhythm, a beat that I've heard before but a bit different. There is something else too …' Felicity hesitated as she knew what she was about to say to Nursey would sound ridiculous. 'There is some sort of singing. I mean, it's not singing like Adele, but I sort of know the tune from somewhere but not the words. And I don't recognise what language it is – not English. But it's there OK.'

'I can hear what you mean,' agreed Nursey, 'and I don't recognise any language either, or a tune that I know. Maybe we can get Kurt to isolate it and do his special stuff on it. He used to analyse all kinds of weird noises when he worked for that big German fridge company, oh, what were they called? Yes, Naff. That's them.'

'There is one other way,' whispered Felicity, almost as if she didn't want Nursey to hear it.

'Oh, go on. I am all ears,' Nursey replied, smiling. This was exactly what she had hoped for.

'This is going to sound weird I know but I promise you it's true. You remember I had those Irish dance lessons last year?'

'Yes, I do,' replied Nursey, 'and I remember you were pretty good at it too. I was very sad when you didn't keep them going.'

'Dad didn't have the money and it was a long way to go,' shrugged Felicity. 'I loved it but had to give it up. However, we had a fantastic teacher and I am sure this rhythm and tune were played in some of our routines and rehearsals.'

'Do you think he'd be willing to listen and try to help us identify it,' asked Nursey.

'Oh yes for sure. But it's not a "him".'

'Alright then, her,' suggested Nursey.

'Well … it's not a her either,' Felicity replied.

'Oh, right, OK, no problem,' said Nursey, 'I suppose we shouldn't be so, er, judgmental in these enlightened times,' with thoughts of all kinds of politically correct issues lying ahead.

'My teacher was a horse.' Felicity paused for this to sink in. Nursey's mouth formed a wide 'O' shape but made no sound for a few seconds until she recovered her composure.

'A HORSE???????' screeched Nursey. 'A horse?? What do you mean a horse? Like a pantomime horse that has real people inside it, right?'

'Urm, no, an actual horse. You know, four legs, a tail and big teeth kind of horse?' This wasn't sounding any better out loud. 'It, I mean, he, is a very special and unique kind of horse.' Felicity felt her face flush and her cheeks burn. She knew that her aunt would struggle with this but it had to be done.

'His name is Horsey Handbrake.'

Nursey nearly fell off her chair.

'Holy Moley, in the name of the sky, how does a horse get called Horsey Handbrake? And whilst I am at it, how does a horse teach Irish dancing?' Nursey's head was reeling. She wanted to believe Felicity – after all how could a nine-year old just make this stuff up?

'He is from a long line of Irish talking dancing horses,' stated Felicity as if this was the most normal thing in the world. 'Not many people know this but they are great dancers and great choreographers. And because they have four hooves, they can tap dance twice as fast as any human who only has two legs. Horsey Handbrake holds the world record for 80 taps a second. That's faster than the fastest human recorded.' She paused to see if her aunt was taking any of this in and then continued, 'even after allowing for the number of legs.' As if that made it any easier to understand.

Nursey looked at Felicity in complete disbelief.

'So, let's say this Horsey Handbrake guy is a great dancer and a great choreographer, and he can talk. How does that help us with this?'

'Well it's quite simple really' said Felicity with a perfectly straight face, 'when he was in Rivertrot ...'

She never got to finish the sentence as Nursey almost exploded with incredulity.

'Rivertrot?? What's that?' she cried.

'It's like Riverdance - but for horses.'

Nursey's jaw dropped even more. She could not comprehend this. Her niece was normal and not, as far as she knew, given to flights of complete fantasy. Her brother was not, as far as she knew, in the business of letting his only daughter take part in dance lessons given by a talking horse who also worked with humans. She did the only thing possible. She left Felicity to continue.

'When we did rehearsals, Horsey Handbrake would always play this music as he said it was a special piece for the chorus. So, every time the chorus came on, this was playing. That's where I recognise it from.

The tap dancing and the music. If we can talk to Horsey he can confirm it and probably a few other things as well.'

Nursey slumped back in her seat. Her mouth and lips moved but no sound came out. Felicity filled the gap for her.

'I told you it was going to sound a little weird Auntie Ange, but it IS true, honest. I wouldn't make it up or lie to you.'

'I'm not doubting you my precious girl, but your old aunt is not familiar with these things. It will take a few minutes to adjust,' said Nursey, recovering her composure.

'So how do we contact this, er, Horsey Handbrake then?' she asked, trying to make it more business-like.

'That's easy' said Felicity, 'he's usually on Trotter or Hoofbook.' Felicity smiled at her aunt as if this was the most normal thing in the world. Nursey came close to fainting.

'Indulge me sweetness, I am only just getting used to Google and the electric interwibble thingy. Trotter? Hoofbook? Do explain.' Nursey was feeling distinctly light headed.

'Horses can't use normal keyboards – their hooves are too big. So, Horsey invented Trotter. You can tap out a message with your hoof on a special horse pad, and it sends it out to everybody who wants to follow you. It's called a *Trot*. There is even a high priority version called the *Galloping Trot*. Hoofbook is for horses to share their holiday snaps with other horses, although I have heard a few are now using it to promote things like shows and what have you.'

'Well if it is just for horses, then how do we access it? Nursey was getting terribly confused.

'There is a special translation app that Horsey published,' stated Felicity.

'Of COURSE there is,' squeaked Nursey trying hard not to sound cynical or sarcastic, but probably failing on both counts. 'And I suppose you have this, er, translation thingy?'

'Well, I do but it's on the phone in your safe,' smiled Felicity. 'If you give it back to me I can send him a message.'

By now Nursey was ready to believe anything. She had started out with a normal niece and now she was communicating with talking dancing Irish horses using a special app on her phone. Whatever next? Flying pigs? Ballet dancing elephants? Little green men in flying saucers with helmets and antennae?

'Ok off you go, here it is' Nursey handed the smartphone over to Felicity. `And where do we meet this Horsey guy?' she asked almost dreading the response.

'Easy peasy,' said Felicity, 'he lives just up the road from here. And he's rehearsing his new show so we can go and meet him at the rehearsal venue.'

'Which is where, exactly?' Nursey enquired, wearily, ready to fly to the moon on the back of a painted clockwork dragon.

'Round the back of the race course, of course. Where else would you get all those horses in one place?' Felicity looked at her aunt and simply smiled. She knew this would be a lot for her to take in. The same thing happened when she told her dad, but after the initial shock, he thought it was really cool.

And there was one other thing Felicity had not mentioned yet as she knew it would completely freak her aunt out. That would have to wait until she met Horsey in person.

Chapter 10

Dougie would never admit it to her in person, but he was missing his sister even though she had only been gone one night. With their dad working odd hours and often being away at short notice, they had come to depend on each other for amusement and entertainment. Of course, she could be really annoying – she was a *girl* after all. She wasn't much cop at football, but she and Dougie rubbed along quite well most of the time with lots of shared interests they had enjoyed when their mum was alive. Their dad had done his best to keep those going – the interest in nature, the simple made-up games they played with him that always seemed to involve a cardboard box and of course reading.

Dougie looked up from the book he was engrossed in as his father came through the front door. He immediately walked over and gave his son a hug.

'What have you been up to then young man?' Brad enquired, taking off his shoes and loosening his tie. Even though most of his colleagues in the detective squad at Severn Valley Police dressed fairly casually, Brad always liked to look smart in a suit and tie as he never knew who he would have to meet during the course of a day.

'I played football with John and Billy in the park for a while. Then Billy's mum made us some sandwiches and we watched a bit of a Harry

Potter DVD. But I didn't really like it Dad.' Dougie shrugged and looked for his father's nod to say it was OK not to like Harry Potter, as everyone in his class seemed to think it was great.

'It's a bit old for you I think Dougie – maybe when you're older you'll enjoy it more but it doesn't matter if you don't like it now. Not everyone is the same,' said Brad in soothing tones.

'Have you heard from Felicity yet?' asked Dougie, trying not to look concerned or interested.

'Not yet son, but I did have a call from Auntie Ange. She says that Felicity has settled in OK and seems to be enjoying it. And she has made some friends with the other girls in her dorm.'

'Will I be able to see this place when we go to collect her? It sounds wicked.' Dougie was regaining his enthusiasm and quickly forgetting about Felicity.

'I should think so Dougie,' replied Brad, 'I'm sure Auntie Ange would be happy to show you round once Felicity has helped her.'

At that point, the phone rang and Brad picked it up, seeing it was his sister's number on the display.

'Hi Ange, what's up,' he said casually. 'Has my daughter solved any mysteries yet?' He still wasn't convinced it was a good idea but once Felicity was hooked on it, there was no way he could disappoint her.

'Actually Brad, she is doing a fantastic job already. We have found something odd going on with the Ministry's music system and Felicity thinks she can help us identify it. Seems she knows, er, someone who can help so we're going to visit later today. I will need to drive her into Cheltenham if that's OK?' Nursey Corners tried to sound a lot more positive than she felt but didn't want to mislead her brother. After all, it could easily turn out to be a complete wild goose chase.

'No that's fine Ange as long as you stay with her. Who does she know in Cheltenham though?' the detective in him asked.

'Apparently, she had a teacher when she took Irish dancing lessons?' Nursey was not sure if she should reveal what Felicity had told her.

'Oh, you mean Horsey Handbrake?' Brad said as if this was perfectly normal.

'Yeah, that's the one. Sounded a bit odd to me but if you know this, er, Horsey, er, person, well then I suppose it's OK,' Nursey was relieved to say.

'Sure – don't be put off. It's a little strange at first but he's quite a character. Although I am struggling to see what he has to do with your music system?'

'I am too, if I am honest, but Felicity sounded very confident. Anyway, I will call you if there are any developments. How's Dougie by the way?' Ange enquired not wishing to overlook her nephew.

'He's fine,' replied Brad, 'like me, he's missing his big sister.' He looked at Dougie and winked. Dougie shook his head vigorously and blushed at the same time.

'I'll be sure to let her know,' said Nursey cheerily and hung up. She turned to Felicity and said, 'OK, we're cleared for take-off Felicity. Let's get going so we can be back for dinner.'

Felicity needed no second bidding. She followed Nursey out to her car, keeping a safe distance behind and looking to make sure that no-one saw them together. She climbed into the passenger seat, did up her seat belt and sat down as low as she could. She didn't see the curtain in the Director's office twitch as they drove off.

It took them a little while to find Horsey's rehearsal room at the racecourse but as they approached, the unmistakable sounds of a fiddle playing an Irish jig told them they were in the right place. Felicity led the way and immediately spotted Horsey with his trademark

blonde mane in a tightly combed quiff. She waited until the music finished and the solo dancer stopped in a triumphant pose.

'OK everyone let's take a fifteen minute break,' she heard Horsey call out and with that he turned round to see Felicity. His face broke out into a huge toothy grin.

'Well if it isn't my favourite pupil,' he said, 'come back to see me. Sure it's grand so it is.'

'And it's lovely to see you too Horsey. Did you get my message on Trotter?' asked Felicity.

'Ah to be sure I did little one and I am delighted to hear from you. Now who is that handsome lady with you?' Horsey nodded towards Nursey with a knowing wink. Nursey could not help but blush.

'This is my aunt Ange, but everyone calls her Nursey Corners.' Felicity said confidently. 'She is from the Ministry of Sleep and we have a little problem I think you can help us with.'

'Now, well, to be sure I am always glad to help you Felicity – and your lovely aunt as well.' Horsey had clearly taken a shine to Nursey.

Felicity explained how they had found the second recording but they didn't know why it was there or who had put it there.

'I think there is something on here that you might know or recognise Horsey,' said Felicity, 'but I want to be sure before we try to work out what is going on. It's a mystery.'

'OK roll the tape!' said Horsey theatrically. He listened carefully to the tune from Nursey's iPhone until it had finished, his hooves tapping lightly in time to the beat.

'So, what do you think it is Horsey?' Nursey interjected, unable to contain her curiosity about the music and about Horsey's abilities.

'I'm almost certain,' began Horsey looking pensive, 'but you'd really need an expert if you want to be 100% sure, that it is the hippos from Rivertrot.'

Nursey's jaw almost hit the floor at the same time as her eyebrows shot up. She took a deep breath and tried to stay composed.

'You know Horsey, for a moment, there I thought you said "hippos",' she said with a nervous laugh.

'Well, Nursey, that's because I did say "hippos"' replied Horsey patiently. 'Specifically, pygmy hippos. The ones we used in the original Rivertrot before they all went to the BBC for more money doing that little swimming thing in between programmes. We had to replace them and it took forever to get the show sorted out.' Nursey's head was swimming with images of swimming pygmy Hippos.

'OK, indulge me here Horsey. I am not as familiar with all this dancing as Felicity is, but I understood that Rivertrot was all about horses? Why would you have hippos as well?'

'Oh that's simple,' smiled Horsey, 'hippos are actually very good dancers, once you get them trained. They have a great sense of timing and when you put a line of them together they're quite impressive. You see we put little hippo shoes on their hooves, a bit like the ones the horses have, so that when they tap dance it makes a fantastic sound.'

'I see,' said Nursey, not really seeing at all, 'so how do you know it is these specific hippos? I mean, surely there are others?'

'Oh now Nursey away wit' you, I'll be telling you all my secrets at this rate so I will, but as it's Felicity' he paused to make sure Nursey knew she was getting privileged information, 'if you listen carefully you can tell that the tapping is a little muted. That's because in rehearsals they just wear ballet shoes to save wrecking the stage. Hippos weigh a lot and they have been known to break floorboards. But the real giveaway is their humming. Hippos like to hum and their favourite tune is of course ... the Hippopotamus Song.' Horsey looked at both Felicity and Nursey to see if they knew what this was. Their blank looks said no.

'The Hippopotamus Song is the most famous song written about hippos. In fact, it might be the only one. As you will remember, it has a well-known rousing chorus about, "Mud, mud, glorious mud," that everyone has heard. So, as hippos can't speak English, they just hum it. In hippo. Which is why it doesn't sound like anything else. And as a warm up exercise before we started dancing, they would always hum this and dance to the tune. That's how I know it's them.' Horsey said triumphantly, looking at Nursey as if waiting for applause. None came. Nursey was in a state of shock. She said nothing for about 30 seconds as she tried to process all of this information. Somehow, she had wandered into a world where a talking, dancing Irish horse was explaining to her that pygmy hippos were humming to a famous tune she had never heard. And her niece didn't seem in the least perturbed.

'You see, I told you Horsey would know,' Felicity whispered to Nursey.

'Yes, I am impressed,' conceded Nursey, 'but what has this all to do with the Ministry? And why would anyone go to all the trouble of making a second recording with uh, humming hippos, and then install it on our music system?'

'You have a point there, Nursey to be sure,' agreed Horsey, 'but that's not one I can help you with I'm afraid. I'm just a dancer. Not a detective. Felicity now, well, she's a clever girl and if she's brought you here to see me then I'm sure she can help you figure this out. But if you'll excuse me the show must go on and we have a lot of moves to organise.'

'Of course, how selfish of me,' said Nursey, 'I won't hold you up any more. You've been immensely helpful and I can't thank you enough.'

'Oh now go on will you, sure it was nothing.' Horsey gave what would have been a toss of his mane but the special horse-strength hair spray stopped it from moving. Felicity and Nursey got up to leave and they looked around at the vast stage with the lights and scenery. It was hard to believe this would all be a massive dance show in a couple of months.

'Just one other question if I may before we go?' Nursey turned to Horsey with a smile.

'Sure thing but you'll need to be quick mind,' Horsey replied.

'How did you get to be called "Horsey Handbrake"?'

'Let me show you,' said Horsey with a smile and a wink to Felicity who knew exactly what was coming. Horsey leapt onto the stage and walked off to one side. He nodded to the sound-man who had come back from the break and in an instant the well-known theme from Rivertrot blasted out of the speakers and filled the room. In a flash, Horsey came galloping in doing his trademark leaps and flicking his legs up and across each other at lightning speed. It looked as if he would go careering off the other side of the stage when suddenly his back legs locked and skidded on the boards as he turned himself around, pivoting on his hooves and changing direction without missing a tap. He sped across to the other side and did the same thing again this time coming to centre stage and speeding up his taps until his hooves were just a blur of flashing flesh and the taps merged into each other like thunder. The music hit a crescendo and he threw his head back with a big smile for the audience, putting his front legs on his hind quarters, and taking a bow.

'Bravo, bravo' cried Felicity and Nursey together. Horsey looked extremely pleased with himself, as well he might.

'And that ladies, is my famous "handbrake turn" that nobody else can do. And I might add more taps per minute than even the great Flat Mick.'

Nursey steered Felicity towards the door. She knew that whatever happened next, nothing, absolutely nothing, would ever be the same again.

Chapter 11

They made it back to the Ministry in time for Felicity to go back to her dorm and have a quick wash and brush her teeth before dinner. Nursey took great care to ensure that she parked her car out of view of the main house so that they would not be seen together.

As Felicity came down to the dining room she heard the buzz of children's voices rising up to meet her and hoped she could make an unobtrusive entrance. It was not to be.

'Hey Felicity, where have you been? We've been looking all over for you,' exclaimed Gail as she came bounding up to greet her like a puppy, her hair billowing out behind her. Mandy was just behind.

'Yeah, we needed you for a game of rounders on the lawn. It was great fun – we won, and, we beat the boys!' Mandy enthused, clearly delighted at this modest but important victory. 'You should have seen their faces. It was BRILL!'

'I'm sorry I missed that,' replied Felicity, trying to look disappointed, 'but Nursey had to take me to see the doctor. As I had that funny tummy, they had to call my dad and he wanted me to see a doctor just in case. Even though I was ok mostly. But it's all clear now – no more medicine. It was horrible anyway.' Felicity had worked out the cover story with Nursey in the car and they both agreed this was the last time they could use it. Nobody was going to question seeing a doctor so it stopped any further questions. But from now on, Felicity knew she would have to be super cautious so as not to blow her cover.

'So, apart from beating the boys at rounders, what else have you two been up to?' Felicity asked, keen to divert attention away from herself. They all sat down to dinner and her two friends gabbled excitedly, each talking over the other, to tell her about the game and their exploits around the grounds. Felicity tried to stay focused on what they were saying and nodded or said *'oh'* or *'uh-huh'* at regular intervals. But she was only really thinking about what Horsey had said and how that connected to what she had seen the previous evening when she followed her room-mates outside. She wondered what would happen after lights out tonight.

.oOo.

Nursey took advantage of the general commotion surrounding dinner to find Kurt. As usual, he was in his office. He always seemed to be busy fiddling with some piece of technology regardless of whether it was broken or not.

'You look worried Nursey' said Kurt, 'have you managed to find anything out about the other recording?'

'Indeed I have Kurt. And in some ways, I almost wish I hadn't as it is almost too weird for words. You will struggle to believe this, just as I did, but I assure you it is true as I have witnessed it first-hand,' sighed Nursey, sitting down wearily on Kurt's sole chair for visitors.

'Sounds intriguing Nursey. Do go on,' replied Kurt leaning forward, his engineer's interest aroused.

'It turns out that there is indeed a second recording Kurt and it is different to the one you and I put on the system. There is a definite rumble and I now know what it is,' explained Nursey, trying to find the right words to describe what had happened with Horsey Handbrake.

'The rumble is caused by hippos tap dancing and humming the chorus to the Hippopotamus song.' Nursey paused for this statement to sink in. Kurt was not a man given to extreme reactions but even he could not keep his face straight as his mouth gaped open, trying to form some words that took a while to arrive. He swallowed loudly.

'I see Nursey. Hmmm. Hippos eh? Forgive me for asking this, but how did you find this out? And how can you be certain?' Kurt asked, regaining his composure slightly.

Nursey pondered this for a second and decided that telling him about Horsey Handbrake as well was just going to freak him out completely so she made her mind up to withhold that particular piece of information for now.

'I was able to find someone who, er, knew about these things and it was confirmed as hippos. Pygmy hippos – you know, the cute little baby ones? Not the great big ones you see in Africa' she continued, as if their size made it more believable. 'My source has worked with them, apparently, and was able to identify a specific group of them from the rhythm and sound of their tap dancing combined with the tune they were humming.'

Kurt's mouth flapped again. His orderly engineer's brain was struggling to deal with all of this.

'That's, er, very interesting Nursey,' he finally managed to say. 'If we assume this is correct – and I don't doubt you but I am sure you would agree it is a little strange – then two questions remain.'

'They are probably the same two questions I have been asking myself Kurt,' interjected Nursey. 'Let me guess – how did it happen and, more importantly, why?'

'Correct Nursey. If we can work out how, that might lead us to why and then, very importantly, WHO did it!' Kurt was clearly agitated that his beloved technology and the security system was somehow flawed. It was a real dent in his pride and he was not going to let someone else make him look like a fool.

'I will do whatever I can to help you find out these things Nursey,' he stated very gravely. 'There will be no rest until we do that. You have my word.'

'Thankyou Kurt' smiled Nursey, 'I knew I could rely on you. We'll work on it together and share what we know. But I must tell you that I have a bad feeling about all of this. I cannot shake off the idea that someone inside the Ministry is involved somehow.'

If it was possible for Kurt to look even more surprised, then he managed to do so. He was by nature a very trusting person so it was an even greater shock for him that there could be a mole at the Ministry.

'But why would anyone do that Nursey? There seems no point in just changing a piece of music. Especially if the only difference is the sound of dancing, humming hippos.' Kurt looked baffled and distressed at the same time.

'That's what we have to figure out – and we need to keep it between us for now as we don't really have much to go on. But the entire sleep walking programme could be destroyed if we don't get to the bottom of it,' Nursey reasoned. 'Have you noticed or seen anything unusual lately? Any strange activity on your system for example? Has anyone else had access who could have tampered with anything?'

Kurt thought for a few moments and scratched his head, desperately trying to recollect if he had indeed seen anything unusual.

'Well, this is probably nothing Nursey and I can't say for sure as I wasn't here, but we did have someone come in whilst I was on holiday. The Director said we needed to add some new communications stuff so we could improve our TV coverage. He said something about satellite dishes I think. I know we now have some more channels but I didn't think that would require any changes or system access,' Kurt explained but didn't seem convinced by his own words.

'Who did that work then Kurt?' asked Nursey starting to feel they might be on to something.

'I don't recall now, but it was some firm in Cheltenham that the Director knew. Said they were top notch guys, security cleared and all that. I think he knew them from his time in the Army.' Kurt said with a shrug. Nursey sat up with a start.

'So, when Bertie said our security had been checked over by guys from Cheltenham, maybe that was what he meant? And maybe that is their business card on your board Kurt? I thought he was referring to the Government people as they have a big communications place in Cheltenham, so I didn't make any connection at the time. I wonder ...' but Nursey didn't get to finish her sentence as Kurt had leapt up from his seat and let himself into the equipment room.

He was methodically looking over all the racks of the different boxes with the flashing lights that only Kurt knew about. How anyone could understand that was beyond Nursey so she just watched in silence as

Kurt took his time to check every single item and piece of wiring. There was nothing she could do.

After what seemed an age, Kurt suddenly stood up, banging his head on an overhead rack as he did so and cursing under his breath at the sudden pain.

'Nursey, I think I have found something,' he exclaimed. 'Come and look at this.'

Nursey squeezed past the door and behind the metal racks that held all the boxes to where Kurt was crouched down and pointing. She peered down at the small black metal box that was no bigger than a large mobile phone but had several wires leading from it and multiple small lights which were flashing constantly.

'Looks a bit like a phone to me Kurt,' she said slightly disappointed as from the excitement in his voice she had been expecting something a little more impressive size-wise.

'It's not a phone Nursey but it is making calls of a kind through our systems. And here is the worrying thing. This is not a commercially available device.' Kurt looked at her directly to see her reaction.

Nursey nodded but said, 'And that means what, exactly?'

'I have only seen something like this once before,' replied Kurt. 'And that was when I was doing my national Army service in Germany as a student – we all had to do it. I was lucky and because of my engineering background, I was allocated to the communications division. This is a military specification product which allows people outside to get into computer systems without leaving any trace. No-one outside the Military would be able to get one of these.'

'Is that how the music was replaced then?' asked Nursey with a knot forming in her stomach.

'It would be a key part for sure' agreed Kurt, 'but it does need a dish – like a TV dish. So, whoever installed that dish for the Director, probably put this in as well at the same time. If that's true, then someone outside would be able to control all our systems without us even knowing about it.'

'Good heavens Kurt – that's, that's ... terrible!' said Nursey as the realisation that this was almost certainly done with the assistance of someone inside the Ministry started to dawn on her.

'Let me check one more thing Nursey. Don't go away. I'll be back in two minutes,' and with that Kurt rushed outside leaving Nursey in the equipment room. He came back breathless and wide-eyed.

'It's as I thought. That so-called TV dish isn't for TV. It has been made to look like one but it is a satellite communications dish. That is how whoever outside has done this is able to get access. They send the signals to the dish which then sends them down to this box – look, see this wire here? That goes to the dish – and then into the computer, through this other wire here.' Kurt pointed to all the connections as he described them to Nursey.

'Does that mean they can still do things Kurt?' Nursey asked fearfully.

'Yes it does. But we shouldn't disturb it until we know who did it and why. Otherwise they may disconnect it and we'll never know.' Kurt had composed himself again as he was now thinking once more like an engineer.

'Kurt, I can hardly believe this,' whispered Nursey, 'this must have been done for an important reason. I mean, why go to all this trouble just to have different sleep walking music? It doesn't make any sense.'

'I agree Nursey. It makes no sense to you or me. But it makes sense to whoever put it there. And that's what we must find out next, and fast. Look, it's getting late, you should have some dinner and I'll look back over my records to see if I can identify anything else. Let's talk again in the morning, OK?'

Nursey nodded her agreement and left Kurt's office. As she walked back to the main building she glanced up to see the new dish and wondered why she hadn't spotted it before. She also wondered who she could trust. Her instincts about the Director were strong but if he was indeed behind it, what was it for? Was it just him or were others involved?

With all the other new stuff she had learned today her head was spinning. But there was one more thing she had to do before it was lights out in the dorms. She had to find Felicity. Before anyone else did.

Chapter 12

Gail, Mandy and Felicity were in their dormitory having all changed into their night clothes. Gail had been making them laugh with her stories of life out on the west coast of Scotland, especially in the summer when the midges arrived in force. Felicity was happy to listen as she didn't really want to talk too much about her own home life which sounded very dull by comparison. She really liked Gail, and Mandy, and in different circumstances she would have wanted them as her best friends. But for now, her job was to help her aunt and she knew that being careful was essential, so she was content to let the other two do most of the talking.

The sound of approaching footsteps made them all get under the sheets quickly – not easy given the way that Nursey made the corners so tight. Nursey appeared at the door, smiling.

'Everything OK girls?' she enquired brightly. 'Sleeping OK? No problems with getting out?' Nursey looked at all three in turn.

'It's lovely here Nursey' enthused Gail, 'I can sleep well here.'

'Me too,' agreed Mandy. 'I like the sheets. At first, I thought they were a bit tight and just like the ones my grandad used, but I'm used to it now.'

'Glad to hear it,' Nursey said, 'and what about you Felicity?'

'All good with me Nursey – my bed is very comfy,' came Felicity's happy reply.

'Excellent. But if your tummy gives you any more problems, just come and see me OK?' Nursey looked at Felicity having turned away slightly from Gail and Mandy so they could not see her face as she spoke to Felicity and therefore could not spot the huge wink and silently mouthed *'come and see me when they start to walk,'* in Felicity's direction. Nor could they see Felicity's silent, *'OK'* in response. It was the only way Nursey could think of to ensure that her niece could take the vital next step safely.

'Right then girls, time for lights out now.' Nursey moved towards the door, looked around at all three of them to make sure there were no final questions and bade them *'sweet dreams'* as she pulled the door behind her and flipped the switch, once more plunging the dormitory into darkness. As she walked back to her office she wondered how long it would be before Felicity was able to escape to make their rendezvous. She would find out within the hour.

.oOo.

The pattern of last night repeated itself as Gail and Mandy slipped out of their beds to the sound of the hippo tape. Felicity followed them

as before and saw them disappear around the curve in the path to the same faint glow. But instead of following them, she doubled back to Nursey's office and tapped on the door. It opened at once and Nursey almost hauled her inside before anyone else noticed.

Felicity was surprised to see another person sitting in Nursey's office.

'Felicity, this is Kurt. Kurt is our technical expert at the Ministry and he is the one in charge of the sound system. He knows about the different versions of the music thanks to your discovery and he is the only other person who does. Apart from the people who made it of course.' Nursey spoke quickly and quietly. As if reading her niece's mind, she said, 'And you can trust him completely.'

'OK' Felicity simply said, not knowing what else to say. If her aunt trusted Kurt that was enough for her as she knew Auntie Ange would not risk her dad's wrath otherwise.

'Kurt is sure he knows how the switch was made and we now need to find out why, and who did it. It's possible that someone else here at the Ministry is helping whoever is responsible, so we have to be very, VERY careful now' Nursey continued, 'however, we still need your help one more time.'

Felicity looked at Nursey and then at Kurt. They were both looking at her intently to see what her reaction was going to be. Kurt seemed like a kindly man, serious and deliberate. When he spoke, he had a slight German accent.

'Felicity, you have done very well so far and without your help we would not know what we do. But we will soon need to do this with adults only as whoever is behind this seems to be quite determined to get something – we just don't know what yet. Until then there is one more thing we'd like you to help with, if you are ready to do so?' Kurt's pale blue eyes looked directly at her and she saw that he was genuine and caring.

'OK, what do I have to do?' said Felicity, not wishing to be excluded from anything, but also realizing that her dad would probably have a wobbly if she took a risk.

'We need you to follow your room-mates all the way to where they disappeared last time, and then find out where they went. Once you have done that, report back here to Nursey and me so we can decide what to do next. Do you think you can do that without being seen?'

'I think so,' said Felicity trying not to sound either nervous or too confident.

'We'll be watching on the CCTV,' said Nursey and you have your phone so you can text me if there is any problem.' She smiled reassuringly at Felicity.

'Ok, I can do that,' agreed Felicity, and let herself out of Nursey's office and back into the darkness of the garden. She waited a minute until her eyes grew accustomed to the gloom and she tuned into the silence. Gradually she could make out the curved pathway and the bushes she used as shelter the night before so she followed the edge of where the grass was, moving steadily and silently. As she rounded the curve the faint rhythmic beat of the hippo tap dance could be heard. And now that she knew what it was and recognised the tune they were humming, she was able to follow that until the faint glow of light was visible.

Felicity crept ever closer until she could clearly see the outline of a fairly large caravan. It wasn't quite as big as the ones they stayed in on holiday but it looked to have a door and a large rear window, and double wheels. On top of the roof she could see a small dish like a TV satellite receiver. She was now within ten metres of the caravan and that's when she saw the large silver 4x4 that sat in front of it, with the caravan attached to its tow-bar. It looked very powerful and had massive tyres. If only Dougie was here he would know exactly what it was as he knew everything about cars and caravans from studying them on holiday and in his book.

She crouched down to get right up to the window where the light was and saw it had no curtain. She realised that she could take a peek inside and that anyone there would probably not see her if she was quick. The caravan was within touching distance now and Felicity eased her way along the side until her head was just below the window. The music playing was very clear now and it was definitely the same recording she had heard. She started to think of the hippos and their chorus.

Taking a deep breath and counting herself down in her head 3, 2, 1, she stood up enough to get a glimpse inside the caravan.

To her complete surprise, Mandy and Gail were asleep in the twin beds opposite the window. Each twin bed was made up with a duvet that was wrapped around the base and seemed to envelop the sleeping girls. Apart from that it looked very much like the inside of other caravans she had seen and been in on holiday. This was really strange. Why would her room-mates sleep walk out to a caravan and get into a different bed to keep on sleeping? Felicity didn't risk looking for too long in case they woke up. She was about to turn back to the Ministry building and report to Nursey when she spotted something in the door mirror of the 4x4 that was hitched up the caravan.

Ducking down low again she took a couple of steps nearer to the big tyres of the 4x4 to try and get a closer look as this could be crucial evidence. She paused to let her eyes recover from having looked into the interior light of the caravan. As her focus returned she was able to get a better view of the reflection in the mirror. The driver was wearing a black beanie hat pulled down over his ears and he had a thin face with a long, pointed nose. He seemed to be asleep judging by his wide-open mouth.

Felicity knew she had to get back silently as quickly as possible to tell Nursey and Kurt. She dropped back into her crouched position and started moving slowly backwards away from the 4X4 and the caravan until she was out of the line of sight from anyone in the car or inside the caravan. She stayed low until she had rounded the curve that hid them both from view and then she sprinted back to the door leading to the corridor where Nursey's office was. She paused to catch her breath and to make sure no-one had followed her.

The slight movement of the curtain in the Director's office went unseen by Felicity.

Safely back in Nursey's office, she recounted what she had seen to Nursey and Kurt. Not surprisingly they were both stunned to know that her room mates had been enticed out to the caravan and were fast asleep inside.

Nursey wanted to know all the details about the duvets.

'Well young lady, that is excellent intelligence. I have a feeling I know who might be behind some of this but I need to go back over some old files to check a few things before I draw any conclusions that we might regret,' said Nursey sternly.

'Yes, well done Felicity,' agreed Kurt. 'We'll get that description checked out.' Kurt and Nursey looked at each other. They didn't have a better explanation.

'OK back to bed for you now. Let me digest all of this overnight,' said Nursey, 'and we'll come up with the next step tomorrow. Agreed Kurt?'

'Yes, *wunderbar*. It might make some sense then,' agreed Kurt, wondering how that could be possible. By now, his engineer's brain was in meltdown. 'See you in the morning.'

Chapter 13

Bertie Bedstead had risen early. Having now spotted Nursey driving out trying to hide Felicity from view, and Felicity coming back from where the caravan was parked, he was certain they were on to something. And he was certain they were working together although as yet he didn't know why.

Even without this connection he knew this was not good news. He woke up in the middle of the night thinking about the situation and decided it was time to turn the heat up on Henri DuVay. Bertie retrieved his phone from its safe behind the picture of him, keyed in DuVay's number and pressed the green button to make the call. Henri answered on the second ring.

'Bonjour Henri,' said the Director, although the day was anything but good in his eyes. 'We need to get this plan into action tonight. There are too many loose ends now and it is only a question of time before one of them leads Nursey and her little friend to us.'

'Bertie, don't panic,' Henri assured him, 'we have everything in place. I will contact my people in England to give them the green light for tonight. Nursey won't be a problem for much longer, I promise you.'

'Well, I appreciate your confidence Henri but I've seen too many plans collapse because something unexpected turned up. I want you to go over it one more time with your team here and think the unthinkable. What happens if, for example, your caravan gets a puncture?' suggested Bertie. 'What if Nursey puts up a fight?' Have you thought of that?'

'Of course Bertie, we have the right team to deal with all of that. You must learn to trust me and relax. It will be fine,' purred Henri.

Henri was right of course. Bertie was always worrying about details that were not important and he caused Henri no end of frustration trying to keep him calm. But the reward was worth it and without Bertie's signature the entire plan collapsed so, for now, Henri humoured the Director.

'Right you are then Henri – I will leave it to you completely. There can't be any connection back to me anyway so once the operation is underway, it is all under your control. After everything is taken care of you can send me the agreed code word and we move to the next phase. The one where we make some money,' said Bertie with his enthusiasm returning. 'Radio silence until then.'

And with that he disconnected the call. As he sat at his desk looking out over the grounds of the Ministry he would soon be leaving with a handsome payoff, he tried not to think too much of all the things that could happen. If it all fell apart, then he would blame it on DuVay anyway. He had covered his tracks thoroughly. Or so he thought …

.oOo.

In the main room of the Ministry, breakfast was in full swing when Felicity came down from her dorm, having held back as before so she could put her phone back in its hiding place without being spotted by Gail and Mandy. As she approached the table where they were sitting she noticed that the German boy, Will, was also sitting there chatting to her room-mates. Felicity sat down between them and the conversation stopped.

'Hello Will,' said Felicity brightly, 'how are you? Settling in OK? I see you've met my friends Gail and Mandy already.'

'Yes, I'm fine thank you,' replied Will in his impeccable well-mannered English. 'How are things with you? Gail and Mandy have been telling me about some of the games you play. Sounds like fun.'

'We told Will about our game of rounders yesterday,' chirped Gail in between bites of her toast, 'and that we beat a team of boys.'

'Do you play rounders in Germany Will?' asked Mandy.

'I don't really know for sure,' said Will, 'I live here in England so I don't have much contact with German schools. But I don't think it is a German thing. They are more interested in football.'

'Will's dad works for a big German supermarket,' Mandy said, looking at Felicity to see if she already knew this. 'He's in charge of ALL of them.'

'Wow, that sounds exciting,' said Felicity, 'I didn't know that. We never got on to that yesterday.'

'Actually, it was my grandfather who started the company in Germany many years ago, with just one market stall in Freiburg. He was very good at buying and selling and he was able to offer things at lower prices than others which made it successful. He grew it from there and opened up a proper shop. Then a few more and pretty soon he was all over Germany.'

'Gosh that's AMAZING,' cooed Gail wide eyed, 'how many shops do you have now?'

'I don't know exactly, but in the UK, it is nearly 1000. In Germany and in Europe it's a lot more.' Will tried not to sound boastful but he was very proud of what his grandfather had done. 'You might have heard of it as it has our family name?'

The girls all looked at each other blankly. They didn't know much about supermarkets as their parents tended to do their shopping for them but they knew about ones like Sainsbury's. Gail was first to break the silence. 'What's it called then?' she asked.

'Widl' replied Will, looking to them to see if they recognised it.

Suddenly they all connected to the name they had seen countless times but had never really thought about.

There was a collective intake of breath.

'So, you're Will Widl then?' Mandy said haltingly, not really sure how this all worked – it could have been his grandfather on his mother's side.

Will reached into his back pocket and took out a small wallet. From it he took a business card and passed it to the girls. They had never seen a business card before let alone one carried by a boy their age. They passed it round between them and noted the company logo they were all now familiar with and Will's name, along with his email address.

"Will.e.widl" it said, along with a mobile phone number and the company logo. There was nothing else. The girls all looked at him with wide eyed amazement, not really knowing what to say.

'Er, what does the 'E' stand for Will?' asked Gail, ever the curious one.

'Englebert,' Will replied somewhat sheepishly. 'My mum loves music and when she was younger she really liked this singer called Englebert Humperdinck. She wanted to name me after him. And it's sort of a German name. She also likes Will.I.Am, you know, the guy on the Voice? So, she thought it would be cool to give me a similar one.' Will nodded as he spoke trying to make it look as if he was happy with his mother's ideas.

'Does that mean you actually work for Widl's then?' asked Felicity as she knew that most people who had business cards were employees of someone – or at least her dad had told her that when he got his first card in the Police.

'Oh no, I'm too young but my Dad tells me a lot and he teaches me about business. I look at the figures and he explains to me what they mean. And how to find things out properly on the internet so we can make sure we know what other shops are doing. I think one day he wants me to join the company but he said I would have to start at the bottom like him and his dad.' This was all sounding a bit dull so Will changed the subject quickly and asked,

'What do you all want to be when you grow up?'

Again, they all looked at each other not sure how to answer. None of them had really thought about it too much.

'I'm going to get some more toast' exclaimed Felicity, 'does anyone else want some more?' They all nodded enthusiastically as they had stopped eating for a few minutes whilst all this information sank in. Felicity wanted to avoid having to say her Dad was a detective, as other children often made fun of her or did silly impersonations of what they thought policemen did.

As she was standing at the toaster making sure it didn't burn her toast, Felicity could see Nursey Corners come into the room, scan around and when her gaze fell on Felicity, start to walk towards her.

'Everything OK with that tummy of yours now Felicity?' asked Nursey, mainly for the benefit of the others within earshot.

'Oh yes Nursey, all OK now thank you,' smiled Felicity, 'those tablets worked fine.'

'And you're sleeping OK?' Nursey continued.

'I am, yes, very well, thank you.'

'Glad to hear it. I'll just go and check with the others and then I must get back to my office.' Nursey said the last few words very deliberately and raised an eyebrow in Felicity's direction to convey the real meaning which was that she wanted Felicity to come and see her soon.

Felicity picked up what Nursey meant and just nodded in response. She knew that Nursey would have a plan worked out and needed to share it with her. All Felicity had to do now was to work out how to give Gail, Mandy and Will the slip without having to resort to using her tummy as an excuse. She headed back to the table with four slices of hot toast. Her room-mates grabbed one each as did Will, and applied butter and jam. They all munched contentedly on the toast.

'What are you going to do today Will?' asked Felicity.

'I thought I would try out the electric piano keyboard. It looks like it has some nice effects,' he replied.

'Can we come with you?' asked Gail, 'I'd like to have a try as well.'

'Me too' said Mandy.

'Of course you can,' agreed Will. 'We can maybe form a band?'

Gail and Mandy looked at each other and then Will, nodding enthusiastically.

'What about you Felicity?' said Will, not wishing to exclude her.

'I'm tone deaf,' said Felicity, 'I'd just be in the way so I think I will read my book or take a walk in the garden. But I'm keen to hear what you come up with. Maybe you can play it for me later?'

And with that, the three budding pop idols all headed off to the room with the musical instruments. Felicity smiled to herself. At least she wouldn't have to come up with a cover story now. Once they had all disappeared Felicity made her way to Nursey's office and knocked quietly. The door opened and Nursey beckoned her in.

'Here's the plan for tonight,' said Nursey in her business-like way, then suddenly remembered it was her niece. 'But before that, do you want a drink of anything? Or a biscuit?'

'A biscuit would be nice,' grinned Felicity, taking one of the cookies from the jar that Nursey offered her. 'Mmm, these are yummy.'

'Yes, I got them in Widl's – they do really good biscuits,' agreed Nursey.

'Oh really – that's a coincidence. Will is a Widl. I mean his name is Widl. Will.e.widl it says on his card,' Felicity told Nursey.

'You mean the German boy who is on the bed wetting programme is called "Will E Widl"?' asked Nursey as Felicity burst out laughing. 'I suppose it does sound a little funny but when you say it like the Germans do, it sounds different so maybe his mum didn't realise what it was like in English. Let's just call him Will shall we as we don't want the others making fun of him.'

'He's very nice,' said Felicity, 'and I like him, so we'll stick with Will then.'

'Right – good. The plan then?' Nursey looked at Felicity to make sure she was focused.

'Tonight, once your two room-mates come back in from their little stroll out to the caravan, I want you to send me the code word in a text. Then I will know the coast is clear. Once they're back in bed, I am going out to that caravan to have a look inside and see what it is that makes them come to it. Somehow there has to be a link between the caravan, the music being switched and those duvets. I'm certain the evidence will be in there.'

'What will you do then' asked Felicity with a little worry in her voice.

'I'll come back here of course. And then in the morning you, Kurt and I will go over what I have found and look for the connection. Once we have it, we'll find out who is behind all of this and confront them.' Nursey had that steely look in her eye again and Felicity knew she would be not deterred.

'You will be careful won't you Aunt Ange? I don't want anything to happen to you and if it does, I will call my dad right away.' Felicity tried to sound very serious and grown up but inside she was nervous. She twirled a strand of her hair around her fingers repeatedly and chewed her lower lip whenever she felt a little unsure of herself.

'Right then, we're agreed?' Nursey smiled at Felicity and gave her a hug.

Felicity hugged her back as hard as she could and went off in search of the next winners of *Britain's Got Talent* somewhere in the Ministry music room. Somehow, she didn't think she would find *Girls Aloud*.

Chapter 14

The rest of the day had passed uneventfully in a gentle haze of games, books, music, food and walks around the gardens. By bedtime, Felicity and her two friends were quite tired and had no trouble in getting to sleep. Nursey had done her normal rounds before lights out, and had given Felicity a knowing wink and a smile to remind her of their plan. Felicity only hoped that she would actually wake up when Gail and Mandy returned from their nocturnal wander.

She need not have worried. As the two girls came back to the dorm, Gail bumped into the door, causing it to bounce off the doorstop in the floor with a loud squeak of its hinges. Whilst this was enough to wake up Felicity it wasn't enough to disturb Gail or Mandy who climbed back into their beds and continued to sleep as if nothing had happened. Felicity reached for the phone she had hidden under her pillow earlier and sent the agreed text message to Nursey. A few seconds later the reply arrived letting her know that Nursey had received it and was about to start her part of the plan.

There was nothing else that Felicity could do now until morning. She tried to get back to sleep so she would be ready to find out from Nursey if the mystery of the caravan had been solved. She wished she could be with her aunt as this was the most exciting bit but she also knew that her dad would have a hissy fit if he thought she was out and about in the dead of night. Soon, she drifted off to sleep vaguely aware of the faint light from Lottie's dorm just down the corridor.

.oOo.

Nursey had seized her phone when Felicity's text arrived. *'Yes,'* she thought to herself, *'now we can find out what is going on here at last.'*

The excitement of unravelling the mystery of the sleep walking girls was tempered by a feeling of apprehension that there might be more to this than she could cope with. All kinds of questions rattled around her head but she knew that only resolute action would uncover the truth. Nursey put on her lightweight quilted jacket as it was cool outside and put a torch and her phone into the pockets. She turned off the lights in her office and waited a few minutes to let her eyes become accustomed to the darkness. Walking slowly but purposefully she reached the door, and opened it silently, pausing to see if there was any movement. Everything was still and quiet as always.

Nursey quickly crossed the gravel path and on to the grass to reduce the sound of her footsteps which might alert anyone to her presence. Following the line of the path and staying close to the foliage of the large rhododendrons she quickly got within sight of the caravan. Even though she had been told about it, she was still surprised and shocked to see it. How could it have got in without them noticing? Then she remembered the small box in Kurt's computer room. Kurt had said that whoever had put it there could change the music without anyone at the Ministry noticing. This meant it was highly likely they had also accessed the gate control system to let the car and caravan in. *These were not coincidences,* she concluded.

But there was no time to figure this out now. She had to get to the caravan before anyone spotted her. She was now just behind it and could see that there were still some lights on inside. She could also see that the large 4X4 that Felicity had described was also still there with its tow-bar attached to the caravan.

'They must be planning to leave again tonight,' thought Nursey. She knew she had to act quickly.

Taking a deep breath and summoning all her resolve, she approached the caravan and opened the door. Nothing – no response. Nursey stepped up into the inside of the caravan and looked around. It was quite spacious –it had a kitchen, what seemed to be a loo, and a seating area at the rear that also doubled as a dining area.

Looking beyond the loo, she could see some twin beds and she stepped slowly towards them.

They had been slept in. Her expert trained eye quickly noted many details but she was particularly focused on the duvets that were arranged on each bed. They were seemingly attached to the sides and end of the bunk beds without actually being tucked in. She examined the edges of the duvet covers and felt something hard but flexible along the hem of each one. Nursey pulled the duvet back from the bed and although it at first resisted, it came away in her hand.

There seemed to be a strip of something sewn into the cover all the way along the edge of it. It was easy enough to bend but also quite stiff. Nursey turned it over and around to see what it was and as she did so the edge of the cover dropped towards the bed and quickly attached itself to the side.

'Of course' she almost said out loud, *'it's magnetic.'* It was one of those flexible plastic strips that were used to make fridge magnets and now it was being used to hold the duvet in place around the bed. *'Rather a neat idea,'* she mused wondering what this had to do with the girls sleepwalking. Her thoroughness led her to check the labels – always a useful source of information. When she exposed it from the

inside seam of the cover it simply said *'Made in France by DuVay Duvets'* along with the usual symbols for washing and drying.

Nursey stood there for a few seconds trying to make sense of all these snippets of information. What was so special about this that someone would go to the trouble of infiltrating the Ministry systems and bringing a caravan in without anyone knowing? Whoever had done this clearly had some other purpose she had yet to determine. *'I'll have to speak to Kurt again tomorrow,'* she thought and let the duvet fall back on to the bed. She turned to get out of the caravan.

There was a loud sound of the caravan door closing quickly followed by footsteps on the gravel and then the noise of the engine of the 4X4 being started up. Nursey took the four steps to the door only to find it locked from the outside. She shook the handle hard but it wouldn't budge.

`Hello, let me out at once!' she cried out thinking and hoping it had been closed by accident. `LET ME OUT' Nursey bellowed at the top of her voice but there was no response. And then with a lurch the caravan

started to move, gathering speed down the driveway towards the large wrought iron gates of the Ministry, throwing Nursey off balance and on to a bunk. As the caravan approached the gates, they swung open and the 4X4 smartly pulled the caravan through them and on to the road, accelerating as quickly as the narrow roads would allow.

Nursey managed to recover her balance to look outside to see where she was going but it was too dark. She quickly realised that she had been kidnapped by whoever was behind the mystery. Her suspicions that someone on the inside must be helping were roused but she could not think who. Somehow whoever was driving knew she would be in the caravan that night. And whoever that was, must be in cahoots with the mole in the Ministry.

Nursey reached for her phone to try and make a call back to the Ministry and alert Kurt. She swiped it to open the menus and tapped on Kurt's entry to contact him. Nothing happened. She tried again. Again, nothing. No ringing. She could see that she had a signal so that wasn't the problem. Perhaps her credit had run out? 'Aha,' she thought, 'I can still call 999', so she brought up the key pad, tapped in 999 and pressed send. Nothing happened. Nursey was starting to get annoyed and slightly worried. Then the penny dropped. Her calls were being blocked somehow. If these people were clever enough, and determined enough, which it seemed they were, they would have the ability to block a phone signal. Nursey realised with dread that there was nothing she could do but wait until the caravan stopped.

However, the caravan didn't stop. It kept on going along dark country lanes. Surely at some point they would have to go through a town where she could perhaps see someone and raise the alarm. But as she thought about this, Nursey realised that this would be impossible from inside the locked and moving caravan. So she resigned herself to a long night. At least there was a bed … and a loo.

Chapter 15

Even though Bertie had said that Henri DuVay could call him anytime, he was still a little grumpy when his phone rang about 11pm with the Frenchman's number showing on the display. He pressed the answer button but said nothing.

'It's done,' came the soothing voice of Henri, 'Nursey will be out of your hair for a couple of days Bertie.'

'Excellent. And you're sure she will be OK – there is no need for anyone to be hurt?' questioned Bertie. Even though he knew that Henri would be true to his word he wasn't so sure about the people Henri used to carry out some of his more secretive work.

'She is in very safe hands and will be well looked after Bertie. You have my word. Now, when will you be taking those contracts to the procurement team? We need to get this moving.'

'You just leave that with me Henri – you have to trust me now and you have MY word. Those documents will be delivered tomorrow morning by hand to the right people.'

Bertie tried to sound reassuring to make sure that Henri didn't press him too hard on the details. Bertie was calling in a big favour from some of his former fellow officers who were still working in the commercial part of the armed forces and he didn't want Henri to be aware that there was nothing actually agreed in writing yet. Still, he was feeling confident that his old charm and the promise of a good

deal for everyone would ensure the successful conclusion to years of patient planning. If this worked out, soon the British Army would be free from the tyranny of making beds and folding sheets to impress drill sergeants. But Bertie didn't want to think too far ahead so he was completely focused on securing this first contract.

'I want another progress report tomorrow afternoon Henri,' demanded Bertie, 'call me at 17.00 hours without fail.' He ended the call and turned over in his sheets – secretly he was quite fond of the traditional bedding but, money was money and a deal was a deal.

.oOo.

The next morning was bright and sunny and the light streaming through the dorm window was enough to wake Felicity up before her two room-mates who were still sound asleep. Felicity felt under her pillow for the old phone and checked the time. It was 7 am. She wasn't due to see Nursey until 8 but she knew her aunt would be up and about, getting ready for her rounds and supervising the children at breakfast. She decided to slip out before her friends woke up and pay a visit to Nursey to get the news from the previous night as her curiosity was rapidly getting the better of her.

Felicity tiptoed quietly into the bathroom to have a quick wash and to change into her day clothes – her usual jeans, well-worn trainers and a sweatshirt style top. Checking that Gail and Amanda were still asleep she quietly opened the dorm door and carefully closed it behind her. Felicity listened at the door for a few seconds to see if there were sounds of either girl waking up but there was only silence. She moved softly but quickly along the corridor and to where Nursey's office was.

The door was closed. Felicity tapped gently on it. There was no response. She tapped again but still nothing. As quietly as she could, she turned the door handle knowing that Nursey didn't lock her office. Felicity poked her head around the door to be greeted by an empty

office. Her aunt's outdoor coat was not on its usual hook behind the door so Felicity realised that Nursey had gone out wearing it, probably last night as the air outside now was warm enough to make a coat unnecessary. As always Nursey's desk was a model of tidiness and order which meant that Felicity could see the charging cable for Nursey's phone on the desk, but no phone. She must have taken it with her. But where was Nursey now? Surely, she would have returned long ago. Perhaps she was having a little bit of a lie-in after a late night?

Felicity decided to send her a text from her phone. Whilst she was waiting for the 'ping' to say there had been a reply, she went outside to have a look around the garden to see if maybe Nursey was just out enjoying the sunshine and a moment of quiet before the chaos of dozens of children clamouring for breakfast descended on her.

She followed the gravel path she had taken the night before and could clearly see adult sized footprints in the grass, highlighted by the fine dew that had fallen in the night. They had to be Nursey's. Following the footprints, she came to the point where the caravan had been parked attached to the large 4x4. Nursey's footprints stopped at the edge of the grass and on the gravel Felicity could see the tyre tracks from the caravan. She also noticed that there was slightly muddy patch on the grass just ahead of where the caravan had been with other much bigger tyre marks. This would have been where the 4x4 had stopped and maybe turned. But of the caravan and the 4x4 there was no sign.

And worryingly, there was no sign of Nursey. No response to Felicity's text. No-one in her office. Only the catering staff were in the breakfast room. Felicity was now getting more than a little concerned about her aunt.

This was not like her at all. She checked around the Ministry building and the grounds near it one more time but Nursey had vanished. Her mind was racing now - what to do? She had to tell someone but who?

As she stood outside trying to make her mind up, there was the sound of footsteps crunching in the gravel. Felicity's heart pounded as she thought it might be Nursey, but she turned to see the figure of Kurt striding towards her.

'Good morning young lady,' he greeted her cheerily, 'what brings you outside at this time of the morning? Couldn't sleep? Well, you're in the right place then!' Kurt laughed at his own joke but saw that Felicity was not laughing – she was quite agitated about something.

'It's Nursey. I think she's gone. She was going to check on that caravan last night and we were supposed to meet again this morning but I can't find her anywhere. Have you seen her?' asked Felicity her brow furrowed with concern and puzzlement. She was chomping on her lip and twiddling her hair.

'I'm afraid I haven't seen Nursey this morning Felicity – let's see if she is in her office, shall we?' said Kurt trying to sound calm but he too was starting to feel a little worried.

'I've already checked there – she's not there and her phone and coat are gone,' snapped Felicity annoyed that Kurt would think she hadn't looked already.

'Ok, well let's try her phone then. If she has it with her, we can ask.' Kurt took out his own phone and in a couple of well-practised swipes called Nursey's number. He held the phone to his ear looking around him as people do when they are waiting for a connection. After about thirty seconds he looked at Felicity. 'Hmmm, nothing happening. That's odd. I'll try again.'

Kurt tapped the redial button and waited again to see if the call would connect. He waited about a minute before turning to Felicity. 'Well, that IS unusual. If she had no signal we'd get voice mail, but it simply not connecting.'

'I'm getting quite worried about her Kurt and we need to find her to hear what happened last night when she went to the caravan. I hope

nothing has happened to her – the caravan has gone.' Felicity was displaying some of the assertiveness that both her dad and Nursey used when they needed to make things happen – it ran in the family.

'Right, let's go back to my office Felicity and I can run a few more checks from there. Don't worry, Nursey will be fine. She can look after herself – she was in the Army for many years and nobody messes with her, trust me.' Kurt wished he believed his own words but for now they had nothing to go on so it was time to dig a little deeper.

Kurt sat down at his computer and motioned to Felicity to sit in his visitor chair. He tapped some commands into the keyboard and peered intently at the figures appearing on the screen which Felicity could see but not understand.

'It looks like whoever installed that black box is also able to operate our gate security system. The gate was opened at 10.14 pm last night and closed at 10.16. Let me just check the CCTV.'

Kurt used his mouse to scroll around the screen to a different menu and very quickly located the feed from the camera overlooking the main gate. He found the footage from the previous evening and swiftly located the exact time when the gate had been opened and closed.

Kurt studied it intently as the quality wasn't very good due to the lack of light. But as he played the recording, the caravan and the 4x4 towing it were both visible as they were captured on a few frames. There wasn't a clear view of either so he could not see the number plate or the make, just that it looked to be silver. He stopped the frame at the point the caravan passed the camera. With his mouse, he zoomed in to the window. And there, just about visible, was the outline of Nursey Corners.

'Oh no,' he exclaimed.

'What it is?' cried Felicity coming around behind the desk to look over Kurt's shoulder. He just used the mouse pointer to direct Felicity's eyes to the grainy but unmistakable image of Nursey inside the caravan. Felicity gasped loudly and her hand flew up to her mouth.

'Is that Nursey?' she turned to Kurt and asked. Kurt nodded his head.

'It looks like it. Can't be 100% sure but the timing fits and we can't find her now. Unless I am very much mistaken Felicity, Nursey has been kidnapped.' Kurt didn't know how to say it so he just kept his voice as calm as he could.

Surely this could not be happening? Who would kidnap Nursey? And why?

Felicity was very upset and started to cry a little. 'She's my aunt. We have to find her Kurt.'

'Oh my god,' he said aghast and shocked. 'I had no idea. Of course we must find her.'

'My dad's a policeman. A detective. We have to tell him and get the police looking for her now. He'll know what to do,' said Felicity regaining a little of her composure.

'Yes, yes, we must, of course, good idea,' stammered Kurt losing a little of his.

'But we don't know where she is or who took her. She could be anywhere.'

The colour drained from Kurt's face as he realised the impact and implication of what he was saying. He could see how upset Felicity was but he was also amazed and impressed at how she was still able to focus on doing something that would help her aunt. With a detective for a father, some of that had obviously rubbed off on her.

'You call your dad – you can use my phone – and I have one more thing I want to check out that might help.' Kurt turned to his computer screen again and started typing furiously.

.oOo.

Brad Frampton was sitting in his kitchen, savouring his first cup of proper coffee, listening to the radio news and enjoying the rare moment of peace and quiet before Dougie came thundering down the stairs. Whatever else Dougie was, subtle was not part of it. You always knew when he was close by. It was also a day off from the normal crazy hours he had to work as a senior detective. All kinds of murky goings on had to be dealt with by the detective team under his command – things that most people outside the police would not believe could actually happen. But if there was one thing his 20 years on the Force had taught him it was never to be surprised by what people could do.

His mobile rang and he sighed. Even though he was off duty today, as a Detective Chief Inspector, he was always on call. He looked at the number on the display and it looked similar to the one that Ange used when she called him from work.

'Brad speaking.' He didn't give his full name or rank unless he knew exactly who was on the other end of the phone, especially as his number was only known to very few.

'Dad, something's happened to Auntie Ange. She's gone. She was supposed to meet me this morning but she wasn't there and when I went looking for her I saw Kurt and he checked the CCTV and he thinks she's been kidnapped.' Felicity blurted it all out without stopping for breath.

'Whoa, hold on Felicity, slow down a bit. How do you mean Ange has been kidnapped?' His anxiety levels shot up as that bad feeling he had at first came back to haunt him. 'Are you OK?'

Felicity recounted all the things that she and her aunt had discovered and the plan they made, and how Kurt had spotted Ange in the caravan. Her father listened intently his heart sinking. Kidnapping was rare but they had a well-tested routine in the Force to manage these situations. He just never expected it to happen to him and his sister. His mind was racing as Felicity spoke and his first thought was to get her out of the Ministry and back to safety. If they, whoever they were, had taken Nursey they could take Felicity.

'Ok my precious, here is what we're going to do. I need you to be very brave but most of all VERY careful.' And he started to explain to Felicity how they would get her aunt (and his sister) back safely. At the end of the call he said, 'You are going to be OK. I won't let anything happen to you. I love you lots so we'll speak soon. Make sure you keep your phone on and charged up.'

'Of course I will Dad. I love you too.' Felicity rang off and looked at Kurt. He seemed more confident and about to tell her something positive.

Chapter 16

Bertie Bedstead sat back into his First Class seat on the West Country train to Bristol. Everything seemed to be going to plan at last. The staff at the Ministry had been told that Nursey would be taking a couple of days off to visit relatives so that her absence would not raise undue concern.

He had completed and signed the recommendation section on the procurement contract which would place the order with Henri DuVay's company. Despite having left the Army a few years ago to take up his current position at the Ministry, he had maintained close contact with senior officers who, like him, had been asked to help with selecting new equipment for the Army. Whilst bedding was not the most glamorous purchase, certainly not compared to tanks and guns, it was still essential to the well-being of the soldiers. Crucially, it was also a lot less visible to outside scrutiny and so he was able to gently steer the decision towards DuVay's company. The one in which he held a significant, but hidden, share.

When his phone rang to disturb his thoughts, he looked at the number and saw it was from the Ministry of Sleep.

'Bedstead speaking,' he said softly, so as not to arouse the irritation of his fellow passengers.

'Good morning Director, it's Kurt here,' came the slightly accented voice of his technical manager.

'Kurt, I'm on a train at the moment so I can't really speak. What's the problem?' Bertie tried to sound bright and breezy but inside he felt distinctly nervous. Kurt didn't call him unless there was some major glitch that he couldn't handle.

'It's Nursey Corners, Director. I'm afraid she has gone missing.'

Bertie suppressed a smile – of course she had. He had arranged it.

'But she's on holiday today Kurt so I'm sure you're mistaken. Did you not see the email I sent to everyone yesterday? She wanted some time off to visit her family.'

'I'm sorry I didn't see that one yet but it's worse than that Director. I'm sure she has been kidnapped.' Kurt's tone left Bertie in no doubt that he was completely serious and if Kurt was one thing, it was serious – and thorough.

Bertie's mind was racing. He of course knew that Kurt was correct but he had to pretend that he was surprised and of course concerned.

'Good gracious Kurt – that's terrible. Why do you think she has been kidnapped?'

'We have some CCTV footage that clearly shows her being driven away in a caravan. She has been missing since last night but we only discovered it this morning,' confirmed Kurt, waiting for a response from Bertie, which took a few seconds to come.

'Have you called the Police?' asked Bertie, trying to stay calm and not panic Kurt into doing something rash.

'Not officially,' replied Kurt, 'It turns out one of the children on the sleep walking programme has a father in the Police force so she has spoken to him. He is Nursey's brother apparently.'

Bertie cursed under his breath. Why had he not realised that the new girl who had been so nice to him was Nursey's niece? And how had DuVay's man not switched off the CCTV cameras as he had been instructed? This brought a new twist to his plans. Once the Police arrived at the Ministry he would have to return there and supervise everything, which meant his plans to get the contract into the Army buying systems today was at risk.

'Listen to me Kurt. We don't want the bad publicity that would come from the Police being on site asking lots of questions. The media would get hold of it very quickly and all the hard work we've done to build up our reputation would be wasted. Just keep working with this family policeman until I get back. I'm sure there is a simple explanation or there has been some mistake somewhere and Nursey will show up soon.' Bertie hoped this would buy him enough time to deliver the contract and get back before things got completely out of control.

'OK Director, we'll do that. I'm sure you're right, everything will be fine,' said Kurt and with that he hung up.

Kurt turned to Felicity and frowned.

'The Director has asked us to work through your dad for now and not call the local Police. He thinks Nursey is OK.'

'But she's been kidnapped Kurt,' insisted Felicity. 'She might not be OK. We don't know who did this. They might be really nasty.'

'Yes, you're right they might be but we don't know so we must stay positive. For Nursey. When will your dad be here?'

'He said about 9.30. He's got to get my brother out of bed and have breakfast, then drop him here so he can go to the Police station where they have all the computers and stuff,' replied Felicity.

'Right, in that case we should get some breakfast as well,' smiled Kurt trying to look more positive than he felt.

'This could be a long day so we should eat whilst we can.'

He looked at Felicity and saw that she was trying to be brave and not appear too concerned but he also noted the faraway look in her eye that said her mind was elsewhere. She was only nine years old after all and would not have experienced anything like this before. Very few people would. They walked off to breakfast together but he let her go ahead of him. As they got to the main building he paused for a moment.

'Felicity – we should keep this to ourselves for now as it would probably upset the other children. The staff think Nursey is on holiday so let's keep it that way until we know for sure what's going on. I think that's the best thing, don't you? We can work with your dad once he gets here and let him decide what to do – this will be out of our hands soon.'

Felicity looked at him and saw that he was being completely genuine and was obviously concerned for the safety of her aunt. And yes, there was no point in telling her friends as they would only bombard her with questions she couldn't answer and probably make things worse. It was also the advice her Dad had given her so she felt a lot more comfortable now that Kurt was involved. Plus, she was secretly looking forward to having Dougie around. Even though he could be a bit irritating, like all brothers, he had a knack for spotting things that other people missed so with any luck they could uncover some clues that would help their dad find Nursey soon.

.oOo.

Brad and Dougie approached the formidable entrance gates of the Ministry in their modest eight year-old car. Brad lowered the window and pressed the intercom button. A CCTV camera swivelled in their direction.

'I'm here to see Kurt?' said Brad, not wishing to use his official rank as he didn't know who would answer.

'Yes of course Chief Inspector, I'm Kurt. Welcome to the Joshua Turner Institute. Please follow the gravel drive to the main house and park around the back. You will see a small stone building on your right. That is my office. I'll meet you there.' The gates swung open and Brad eased his car forward and drove at a gentle pace to the main house.

'Is this where Felicity has been staying Dad? And where Auntie Ange works? It's amazing!' said Dougie from the back seat.

'It is fantastic, isn't it? How the other half live eh?' Brad's voice wasn't envious. He knew there was no way that he or anyone he knew could ever attain this kind of wealth, but it didn't bother him that others had. Each to his own, was his motto.

'Remember what we discussed Dougie? Aunt Ange is Nursey Corners here and it seems everyone just calls her Nursey. And only Felicity and Kurt know what has happened so don't say anything to anyone else until we figure out a bit more. And you're here because?' Brad left the question hanging as he wanted to see if Dougie had memorised the cover story they discussed over breakfast. Brad had explained to Felicity that she would have to look after her brother today whilst he went to work on his day off.

'I'm here because you had to go into work and there was no-one to look after me and Kurt has said I could help him with the computers for a day,' Dougie recited perfectly. Brad looked at his son in the rear-view mirror and smiled at him. He knew Dougie would be absolutely fine. He found the parking space that Kurt had described and knocked on Kurt's door. Kurt opened it and invited Brad and Dougie to come in. It was all a little cosy as Felicity was already there occupying the sole spare chair but Kurt said he would get an extra seat for Dougie.

'Good to meet you Chief Inspector,' said Kurt with a slight bow of his head and a warm handshake.

'Please, call me Brad, everyone does. And it's good to meet you as well Kurt. I understand you are in charge of all the technology at the Institute – or should I call it the Ministry?'

'Either is fine Brad, but most people refer to us as the Ministry,' said Kurt relaxing visibly. He wasn't used to dealing with senior detectives and it was a relief that Felicity's father seemed perfectly normal.

'OK, so take me through everything from the time you first noticed something unusual to calling me this morning,' instructed Brad, switching to 'detective' mode. Kurt spent the next 30 minutes recounting all they had discovered, showing him the devices that had been installed and the CCTV footage that confirmed it was Nursey in the caravan.

As the grainy picture played Brad felt a sudden surge of anger that someone could have taken his sister against her will, but he tried not to show it – he had to remain detached and professional.

'Just stop it there would you please Kurt' asked Brad, 'I'd like to take a closer look.' Brad took out his reading glasses and leaned towards the screen. 'Yes, that's Nursey all right.'

'Dad,' piped up Dougie who had also been looking at the screen closely.

'Yes son, what is it?' Brad knew better than to dismiss what his son would have seen.

'That car. It's a Mitsubishi Shogun. And the caravan is a Lunar – you can tell by the stripes just under the window.' Dougie just looked at his father and shrugged as if to say, 'well, everyone knows that, don't they?'

'Are you sure? How can you tell? Brad asked, surprised that even Dougie had come up with an identification so soon.

'There was one just like it when we were on holiday. And the mirror is the same as the ones on my friend Billy's dad's car.'

'That's incredible Dougie. Well done son. We can use that to try and track down the people who took Nursey.'

'There are tyre marks outside,' chirped Felicity, 'if we look at those too it might help? You said that you can tell a lot about a car from its tyre marks Dad.'

'You two don't miss a trick, do you?' laughed Brad, 'OK let's go and take a look at the evidence then.' And they all trooped outside and followed the path to where Felicity had spotted the tread marks on the muddy verge.

'What do you think Dougie?' asked Brad.

'They're probably Bridgestone. They make big tyres for cars like the Shogun and the tread is the same one as Billy's dad's car.' Dougie spoke as if this was just everyday knowledge for a small boy but his father knew that Dougie had an almost photographic memory for all kinds of details about cars, caravans and anything that moved.

'They look pretty new to me,' observed Brad, 'the tread is quite deep here.' He pulled out his phone and took several pictures. 'I'll get these analysed when I get back to the station.'

'You could check and see if anyone has sold tyres like this for a Mitsubishi Shogun' suggested Felicity. 'That might lead you to the car and the owner?' Brad smiled wryly. He had been through this with both of his children when they were playing 'detectives' at home and was delighted that although it had been a game, the serious purpose was not forgotten.

'Well that certainly gives us something to go on,' agreed Brad. 'Well done you two.' He beamed with pride at his two kids and thought how much they would have relished telling this story to their mum.

` Now I must get to the station and get some people assigned to this urgently. Nursey has been gone nearly 12 hours now and she could be anywhere.'

'Not exactly anywhere,' Kurt said.

Everyone stopped and looked at him. Felicity had thought he was looking a little pleased with himself and felt that he had uncovered something when he went back into his computer system records.

'I tried to call Nursey's mobile phone and it simply didn't ring. There was no message at all which tells me that it is possible her number has been jammed. The people who took her are almost certainly the same ones who put that box into my room which means they have the expertise and the means to block out calls.' Kurt paused to make sure everyone was with him.

'If her number is blocked, then we can't contact her can we and she can't contact us? Brad enquired, to confirm his own understanding.

'That is correct, Chief Inspector – for calls, yes. However, GPS location services work differently so they may not have blocked that on her phone. So, I checked to see if I could trace her location.'

'And what did you find Kurt?' Brad asked, anxious to get his investigation underway.

Kurt gazed steadily at Brad and allowed the hint of a smile to cross his lips. 'I think I know where she is.'

Chapter 17

Nursey had drifted off into a light sleep on one of the beds in the caravan realising there was nothing she could do. She woke quickly when she sensed that the caravan had stopped and peered out of the window. It was very dark outside and she couldn't make out any details of where she might be.

The sound of the car doors opening and closing put her on high alert. The caravan door opened a few seconds later and let in a rush of cool night air. There was a dark, large, male figure silhouetted in the doorway, wearing a black coat, trousers and shirt. She instinctively took a half step backwards.

'Don't worry Nursey, we won't harm you. Please just step out of the caravan,' the dark figure spoke to her in a faintly northern accent.

'I'm not going anywhere until you tell me what this is all about and who you are,' Nursey retorted, crossing her arms and putting on her most formidable face.

'I'm sorry but that won't be possible Nursey. All I can tell you is that I am acting on instructions from someone else and that you are not to be harmed in any way. Now, if you would please step out of the caravan, we can continue our journey.'

'My brother is a senior detective in the police. He will be on to you by now so you won't get away with this.' Nursey was getting quite ferocious now as her Army survival training started to kick in. But she also knew that it was best not to antagonise kidnappers so she had to play along to some extent.

'We're aware of that Nursey and have taken measures to ensure that it will be a little while before they catch up with us, but by then we will have returned you safe and sound. There really is no reason to worry or be afraid.' The northern voice was not reassuring even though the words were intended to be.

'You don't seriously expect me to believe that do you?' Nursey cried, trying to stay calm. 'You have taken me against my will and THAT is a serious offence for which you will be severely punished.'

'We prefer to think of it as "*borrowed*" you - for a nice little break. Now please step outside and we can carry on.' The black clothed figure stepped aside and beckoned to Nursey to come out.

'I just need to use the bathroom first. If that's OK with you?' said Nursey, her voice heavy with sarcasm. The figure nodded in response and Nursey went to the small cubicle and locked the door. Her mind was racing. How could she get some message to Brad and Felicity about what was going on and where she was? She was pretty sure that Kurt would be involved at some point and would find a way to track her down. YES! That was it. The tracker on her phone. That would lead them to her.

'We will need to take your mobile phone I'm afraid Nursey,' came the northern voice from outside.

Nursey cursed under her breath. Of course, they would have thought of that. That was why her signal had been jammed. She decided the only thing she could do was hide it in the caravan so that they would be led to that location and just hope that somehow, they would be able to find her after that. It was her only chance and she had to take it. She looked around the toilet cubicle and found a small storage cupboard under the basin. She slipped her iPhone into it and made sure it was turned on.

Nursey pressed the flush button and turned on the tap to disguise any noise.

'I don't have a phone with me,' she said as she stepped carefully down from the caravan which wobbled a bit as it did not have its stabilisers in place. She knew her kidnapper would not have the nerve to search her to verify that little fib.

She still could not see the figure in the dark clothes very clearly although she could see he was thin and wiry, with a large pointed nose and thin lips. A beanie hat covered his hair and ears.

'If you could get into the back of the car please Nursey we will be on our way in a few minutes once we have uncoupled the caravan.' He held the back door open for her as she climbed in and settled into the spacious interior behind the driver's seat. The car's central locking system clicked and the door locks all activated at once. She noticed that the windows in the rear doors were darkened like those of a posh stretch limousine used by film stars.

She might be able to see out but no-one would be able to see her from the outside.

She could hear and feel the sounds of the caravan being un-hooked from the car's tow-bar and then the sound of the stabilising legs being cranked into place.

The caravan door closed and the man in the black clothes plipped the car door open, slipped into the driver's seat of the Shogun and adjusted it. He pushed the lock button again and looked at Nursey in the rear-view mirror.

'Please don't try anything Nursey. All the doors are now locked and yours cannot be opened from the inside. We will get to our next destination in a few hours and then you can stretch your legs. There is nothing more I can tell you so please don't ask.' He waited to see if Nursey had accepted this and although she made no sound or movement he could see from her eyes that she knew it was best to just sit back.

The diesel engine clattered into life and the driver pulled away slowly. Nursey peered out through the darkened windows and into the dark night, trying to discern any detail that might be useful. The place had a familiar look to it and as they gathered speed she saw the white rails of the racecourse. A few seconds later they passed the entrance sign – 'Welcome to Cheltenham Racecourse'. This was getting more and more bizarre. They had been here only the day before and it was Horsey Handbrake who had told her about the hippos. Not just any hippos – but *pygmy* hippos. There simply had to be a connection and if anyone could figure it out and rescue her, it was her brother. And his children.

Once again Nursey had to accept what was happening to her and wait for the next stage to unfold. Her fate was in the hands of others and that was something she really did not like.

Chapter 18

The news that Kurt might know where Nursey was, drew gasps of excitement from Felicity and Dougie. Brad was a little more measured in his response although he was inwardly thrilled to learn that his sister might soon be found. He had previous experiences of kidnaps and knew only too well that false hope could cloud thinking.

'Excellent work Kurt and good thinking on the GPS. So, where is she then?' Brad looked directly at him with an expectant look on his face.

'Come and look at the trace on the screen,' Kurt said, 'it looks to me like it is in the middle of the racecourse in Cheltenham.'

Brad, Felicity and Dougie all huddled around the screen on Kurt's desk peering at the map which showed the pulsing red dot that indicated Nursey's phone. Felicity looked at her father.

'That's where we went with Nursey to meet Horsey,' exclaimed Felicity, beaming from ear to ear. 'That must be where they've taken her Dad.'

Kurt swivelled round in his chair to face Felicity, wide eyed.

'Horsey? Who or what is that? Nursey mentioned hippos – pygmy hippos to be exact – but there was no mention of a horse. Although she did say that she had a trusted source.' Kurt was trying to believe everything he was hearing even though every logical part of his engineer's mind told him this was impossible.

'When Nursey and I went to investigate the rumbling noise on the CD, it was Horsey Handbrake who told us it was hippos,' explained Felicity. 'He used to work with them and the sound was them humming the Hippopotamus Song. So, if she has been taken back to Cheltenham, which is where Horsey was, then it's possible there is a connection with the hippos, isn't there?' She looked to her father for a response.

'It's a link we should investigate for sure,' he confirmed, not really sure how he could work all this out but instinctively trusting his daughter. 'We'll get to the bottom of it but first we have to find Nursey. If she is where you say she is I can organise police cars to be there very quickly.'

Brad was keen to regain control of the situation and avoid being slowed down by Kurt's incredulity and logical engineer's thinking. Whatever he was facing, it wasn't what most people would call 'normal'.

'I have to get to the police station now and get things moving, so I will leave Felicity and Dougie with you if that's OK Kurt? They will be able to help much better from here and I can't allow them to be exposed to danger. I will contact you as soon as I have everything sorted. Now if you'll excuse me, I need to get moving.' And with that, Brad, hugged both his children, reassured them they would be OK and that he would recover Nursey. He dashed out to his car and took his police mobile from the glove box and waited for it to connect to the hands-free system.

As he drove down the long gravel driveway to the exit, he made contact with the duty sergeant first.

'HI Bill, it's DCI Frampton here. I need two marked cars to go to Cheltenham racecourse urgently for a possible kidnapping. I'm on my way there now and should be at the gate inside 30 minutes. They're to wait for me there and not move without my command.' He was now in full police mode and was issuing orders that would ensure Nursey was rescued as soon as possible.

'Leave that with me Sir. Anything else?' asked Sergeant William Hurst, who with his 30 years' service was, inevitably, known affectionately as 'Old Bill'. As an experienced copper, nothing much fazed him and he knew that there would be more to come.

'Can you also patch me through to the Super's office please' requested Brad.

Detective Superintendent Jeff Wilson was Brad's direct boss and like the Sergeant, a man of long Police service who had seen and heard most things in his career. Brad wasn't quite sure how he would react but he needed to get the resources he needed to end the kidnapping, including a helicopter if required. Brad was also keen to get as much done before he had to pass the case over to another officer as protocol would prevent him from investigating anything where a direct family member was involved.

'Brad, what are you doing? Aren't you on a day off today?' asked DS Wilson before Brad could get a word out.

'Yes Sir I am, but something came up this morning that I simply had to deal with but now that I know what it is, we're going to need more resources,' explained Brad, knowing that he would not get away with so little information.

'OK Brad, you have my attention. What is it?'

Brad took a deep breath and launched into a summary of the situation, what he had found out so far and what actions he had taken to try and bring things to a quick and safe resolution. The Super listened carefully, asking the occasional question and making no comment about the somewhat odd circumstances of the kidnapping.

'Right Brad, you go to the racecourse and meet up with the uniforms. See what you find and if your sister is safe and well, then that will be a great result. But if for any reason your information is wrong, you know I will have to take you off the case, don't you?' stated Jeff Wilson. He had great respect and fondness for Brad but the Chief Constable would not take kindly to a breach of protocol, especially as a strange case like this would inevitably get out to the press. But he was prepared to allow Brad the chance to rescue his sister as it would only delay things if he had to get another officer involved when time was so short. He would know within thirty minutes and he felt he could justify that to the Chief Constable if he had to.

'Thankyou Sir, I appreciate your support on this. If we're right, we'll have Ange free in the next half hour.' Brad's relief was evident.

Next, Brad called his own team. A new junior detective, DC Kate O'Hara, answered the phone.

'Thought you had the day off Sir,' she quipped. 'Can't leave us alone eh?'

'Something like that Kate' replied Brad. 'I just need you to do some digging for me. It's urgent. Can you check all the local tyre companies to see if anyone has fitted new Bridgestone tyres recently for a silver Mitsubishi Shogun. One of the older models probably.'

'On the case Guv,' replied Kate, 'won't take long.'

'And if you find it Kate, check to see if it has a tow-bar fitted. If it does, trace the owner and get back to me urgently.'

'Sure thing – I'll call you on this number,' and Kate rang off.

Brad was almost at the racecourse now and as he approached he could see the flashing blue lights of two marked police cars sitting at the entrance, parked off to one side. Brad pulled up alongside the BMW and showed his warrant card to the officers. He wound down his window and motioned to the constable to do the same so they could speak.

'Morning Sir,' said the young officer who looked about 25, 'awaiting instructions as requested.'

'DCI Brad Frampton,' Brad introduced himself as the senior officer, 'just follow me. We're looking for a white caravan, possibly a Lunar, and a silver Mitsubishi Shogun that may be towing it. There is a suspected kidnap victim inside. We need to approach carefully as we don't know who the possible kidnappers are.' Brad thought it best not to mention the hippos or Horsey at this stage. 'We got a trace on a GPS signal from a mobile phone that the victim may be carrying and it looks like it could be round the back near the stables.'

The two officers in the BMW nodded, and motioned to their colleagues in the Astra to slot in behind them. Brad stopped at the security gate and showed his warrant card to the private guard on duty.

'DCI Brad Frampton, Severn Valley Police. We have had information that there might be a stolen caravan and car somewhere on the racecourse so we'd like to take a look around.'

The guard looked at him and the two marked police cars with their blue lights still flashing and asked, 'Do you have a search warrant Chief Inspector?' Brad gave him a withering look.

'You've been watching too many cop shows on TV mate. We don't need one so just lift the barrier and let me in. I can always have the Chief Constable call your boss about the security for the Gold Cup if you like and tell him how helpful you have been,' said Brad briskly and looking impatiently at his watch. The jobs-worth security guard understood the hidden meaning in Brad's statement and quickly raised the barrier.

Brad called Kurt to get a better fix on the location of the GPS signal.

'It should be at the far end where all the stables are. Looking at the on-line earth-view, it seems to be behind the grandstand,' came Kurt's disembodied voice on the speakers.

'OK, stay on the line Kurt, in case I need you,' replied Brad.

As they drove behind the main stand, Brad could see what looked to be a stable block but as it was not a race day it was deserted. He felt his heart sink as there was no sign of the caravan or the Shogun. He carried on driving until he could see a tarmac road leading behind the rows of stables. Turning around the end of the building, he saw the white caravan on the grass. There was no sign of the Shogun. The stabilising legs of the caravan were lowered and the curtains were drawn. It did not appear to be occupied.

Brad stopped and got out of his car, deciding it was best to approach on foot. He signalled to the other two cars to do likewise and the reassuring sight of four burly uniformed policemen emerged from them.

'Let's assume there is someone inside,' he said to the four uniforms. 'I will open the door and try to establish if the suspected kidnap victim is there. You two back me up, one on either side and you two hang back in case anyone makes a run for it. OK?

All four men nodded in confirmation.

Brad moved slowly towards the caravan door and stood to one side of it. He glanced at the two uniforms.

'Ready?' Again, they nodded.

Brad banged on the door.

'Open up. Police' he called out.

There was no response from inside. He banged on the door again and repeated the call to open it, but there was still silence. He reached

forward and tried the handle. It turned easily in his hand and looking over his shoulder to make sure the other two coppers were right behind him and pulled the door open fully.

'Police, nobody move,' he shouted, before sticking his head quickly inside the door to take a look.

'Ange, are you there?' he called out. There was no response so he repeated the question more loudly. Still nothing. He climbed into the caravan and started looking around the rest of it. Ange was not there.

Brad came back out and looked at the two young constables, wondering how he was going to explain this.

'Looks like we got duff information guys, nobody there. Let me just check with my source, hang on here a minute,' and he went back to his car where Kurt was still on the line.

'Kurt, are you still seeing the GPS signal from Nursey's phone in the same place?' he asked.

'Yes, it is still there, nothing has moved. Did you find her yet?'

'She's not here Kurt. I have found the caravan that matches the description of the one on your CCTV but the car has gone. It looks like they have taken her somewhere else.' Brad could not disguise the concern in his voice.

Brad turned to the four officers.

'OK fellas bit of a wild goose chase so far but before we leave here, I need to have the caravan searched,' he told them.

'No problem Sir' replied the first officer he had spoken to. 'Anything in particular we're looking for?'

'Yes, a mobile phone, probably an iPhone, turned on with GPS tracking. That's the signal we picked up but the owner isn't there.'

'Should be no problem Sir, we'll have a good look now,' and they set off towards the caravan.

'There's just one other thing,' called Brad and they turned to look at him.

'The person we're looking for is my sister.' The two officers exchanged glances and looked at Brad. Nothing was said but they all understood now the seriousness of the situation.

Chapter 19

Brad sat in his car whilst the uniformed guys went to the caravan. The line to Kurt was still open.

'Kurt, are Felicity and Dougie still with you?' he asked.

'Yes, they are right here Brad. I'll put them on the line for you,' and he handed the phone to Felicity.

'Hi Dad, what are we going to do now if Auntie Ange has gone?' whispered Felicity, almost too scared to say the words out loud.

'Listen carefully – and make sure Dougie can hear this too,' her father responded, as Felicity turned the handset towards Dougie so he could hear his dad as well.

'Everything is going to be fine. We will find Auntie Ange, you can be sure of it. But I have to hand the investigation over to another senior officer now. It's normal police rules that you can't be in charge of anything concerning a direct family member. But that doesn't mean I won't be very closely watching everything and helping other officers and it doesn't mean you can't help me.'

'That's OK Dad, we understand,' said Felicity looking at Dougie, who nodded his agreement. 'If Nursey has been taken to the race course, then maybe Horsey can help us. There might be a connection with the music and the hippos we can't see yet.'

'Wow, that's fantastic – could you get in touch with Horsey and see if he can pick anything up that might be of use to us? You can still contact me with information and I will make sure the investigating officer gets it straight away.' Brad was relieved to see his daughter keeping calm and thinking positively as he knew how fond she and Dougie were of their aunt.

'Yes, I'll send him a message on Trotter now and see if he can tap into the hippo system. They use Hippogram but Horsey knows how to work it.' Felicity was looking at Dougie and he was taking a keen interest in this too. He wasn't quite as aware of the consequences for Nursey as Felicity was.

'You're a star my sweet, what would I do without you?' Brad said proudly.

'Well, you could check the CCTV at the race course. If they came in last night surely something would have been recorded? You might get the registration number?' Felicity suggested, only because she had heard her father talk so many times about these techniques that she almost knew them by heart.

'Already on the case,' said Brad, cursing himself for not asking the security guard when they came in, but he had been confident they would find Nursey so tracking the car was less important. Now, they really did have to find the Shogun as it was their only connection to Nursey.

'Got to go now you two – the uniformed guys have finished checking the caravan.' With that he hung up.

Constable Davidson approached him – as he could now see from the name tag on his hi-vis jacket.

'Any luck Constable?' Brad asked immediately.

'Yes, we've found the phone Sir. It was hidden in a cupboard in the toilet. I've checked the call logs and it seems there were a number of failed calls late last night. Likewise, there were some text messages that didn't leave the phone either. Given that there is a reasonable signal coverage around here it looks like the phone itself was being blocked somehow.' Constable Davidson paused to see if the DCI wanted him to continue.

'That is consistent with the timing and pattern we saw last night and explains why she couldn't contact anyone. I'll ask the people at the Ministry of Sleep to double check. But now that the phone has been left behind, it does look like we have a kidnapping on our hands.' Brad looked directly at the four police officers who all looked at each other and seemed uneasy. Kidnapping was never a nice situation for the Police.

'As the person who has been taken is my sister, I will have to hand the investigation over to someone else. My Super will assign someone now we know what we are dealing with. We'll need to get a forensics team over here to take that caravan apart and we will have to find the car that towed it here, and presumably, has been driven away with her in it.' Brad was very controlled and precise in his communications with his fellow officers but he knew they would understand his deep concern about his sister.

'Can you get back to the security office and get the CCTV records for last night – everything between 10pm and 7 am. We're looking for a silver Shogun towing that caravan in, and then leaving without it. The sooner we find that car, the sooner we know where to look.'

The uniformed officers jumped into their two cars and set off back to the main gate. They couldn't resist a quick blast on their sirens as they sped off.

As Brad sat in his car, his mind racing on what to do next, his phone rang. It was DC O'Hara.

'Hello Sir, I have some news on the Shogun for you,' she said without any pause for pleasantries.

'Go ahead Kate, I'm all ears,' replied Brad.

'We have found a silver Shogun that was fitted with new Bridgestones about 3 months back. It was done by a local company, not one of the big national chains. They remembered the car clearly as most owners of older cars look for cheaper makes, not premium ones. They also remembered that it had a tow bar.'

'Excellent work Kate. Did you manage to trace the owner or get the registration?' Brad asked with some urgency.

'Er, no. The guy who brought the car in paid in cash and didn't need a receipt. They don't keep records of reg numbers either. But they said he was a northerner, skinny guy with a big conk. Their words, not mine Sir …' Kate was quick to make that distinction to ensure she didn't break any rules.

'Ok, that's disappointing. We're still no closer to locating the vehicle. Can you get someone over to interview the tyre fitter to see if you can find anything else that might be relevant?

'DC Tanner is already on his way Sir,' replied Kate.

'Well done Kate, of course I should have known you would do that. That car has to be somewhere so what I need is an APB for it so that we can check all the motorway cameras and all mobile units. They could be headed in any direction so when we get the first sighting we can hopefully narrow the search. Can you put me through to DS Wilson please?'

Brad updated his boss with the news that Ange was not in the caravan, but they had found her phone. He knew he would be stood down from the investigation. The Super told him that Detective Inspector Campbell would be assuming charge of it for now. Brad was pleased about this as DI 'Jock' Campbell was a very competent detective who would soon make Chief Inspector. He liked Jock and they got on well, so Brad knew that if anyone could find Ange, it would be Jock.

Brad caught up with the four uniformed officers at the race course security cabin.

'Any luck on the CCTV?' he asked, looking at Constable Davidson, who seemed to be the more assertive of them.

'Well Sir, it's hard to tell. It was dark of course but we do have images of the caravan coming in. Rather annoyingly there was no number plate on the caravan but we do have one frame of the Shogun leaving around 11.30 pm.'

'Let's take a look, shall we?' said Brad, looking optimistically at the four coppers. Constable Davidson motioned to the security guard who had challenged the DCI earlier. The guard was being much more helpful now.

Their CCTV system wasn't the best but the image was clear enough. It was a Shogun for sure, and there was a skinny male with a large nose in the driver's seat. Brad could also see a dark shadow in the rear of the car that he knew must be Nursey. The guard clicked forward one more frame and the dark shadow was a little more visible. It was clearly Nursey. Brad turned to the other police officers.

'That's her. So now we know she has been taken.' Brad felt his stomach churn to see his sister being driven away by someone he did not know for a reason that he did not understand. Yet ...

'Have we got a make on the number plate?' Brad looked again at the uniformed officers.

'Yes Sir, we've run it through the computer and it is registered to a Walter Braithwaite, with an address on a business park in Cheltenham,' said Constable Davidson looking very pleased with himself.

'So why are you still here then? Get over to that address and find out what our Mr. Braithwaite could be up to!!' Brad was excited now he had a clear identity for the car.

'And get all of this over to DI Campbell as he is now running the show. He can update the APB and with any luck they will show up on a camera somewhere.' Brad exclaimed.

The uniformed officers all trooped out of the small cabin, and Brad nodded to the guard and thanked him. 'That will be a different call from the Chief Constable now,' he smiled wryly at the guard who nodded his appreciation.

As they walked outside, Constable Davidson stopped and spoke to Brad.

'We'll do everything we can to catch these people Sir, and get your sister back unharmed.' Brad nodded his appreciation with a grim smile.

Chapter 20

It was still dark when the Shogun with Nursey in the back seat finally stopped. Nursey had dozed in the back of the car as it was driven through the countryside. They only occasionally passed through villages and small towns, none of which she recognised and most of which were hard to see through the blacked-out privacy glass of the rear windows. The driver had not spoken to her once during their journey. He applied the hand brake and turned off the engine. All was silent. The driver climbed out of his seat and opened the door next to Nursey.

'You can get out now Nursey, we're here. This will be your home for the next few days,' he said calmly, holding his arm out to indicate that she should step out.

'This is not my home and never will be,' retorted Nursey defiantly. 'I demand you take me back at once.'

'I'm very sorry Nursey but that won't be possible, as I have said before,' came the still calm reply. 'It's best you just settle in and make yourself as comfortable as you can.' And as he held the door open, Nursey could see in the faint light of the coming dawn that she was in a caravan park. Well, at least that was what it looked like as there were rows and rows of them parked side by side. Some were of the permanent type that she had seen on the holiday parks her brother took Felicity and Dougie to for holidays, but there were also a lot very similar to the one she was just getting out of. None of them seemed to be occupied as there were no other cars there. She also noticed that the mobile caravans did not appear to have any gas bottles connected. A sure sign they were not being used.

'Please follow me Nursey,' said the driver and Nursey once more noted his faint Northern accent. He nodded towards a single caravan that was parked the other side of what looked like a small office block. As she walked past the building Nursey saw the sign above the door which said, 'Reception' and the above it in large colourful letters another sign proclaiming 'Welcome to the Hippodrome Caravan Park' along with a cartoon-like picture of a smiling baby hippo dressed in blue polka dot pyjamas. Nursey knew at once there had to be a connection – she didn't believe much in coincidences and this was now the third time that hippos had featured in her life in the past two days.

'What's that hippo doing there?' she demanded of the driver. He stopped and looked at her.

'I really can't answer your questions Nursey, I've told you before. I am under strict orders.' He sounded almost apologetic. 'Now please, if you don't mind, come with me,' and he continued past the reception door to a caravan that was very similar to the one she had vacated only a few hours before. He opened the door and turned on the lights – this one was connected up to gas, water and electricity. As Nursey climbed in the caravan felt reasonably warm. They had been expecting her so this was not some random event, it must have been carefully planned. Her mind was racing to try and piece together how this could have happened but there were too many missing components. It all seemed to be a huge, moving jigsaw puzzle in which she was the main part.

'Please, make yourself comfortable Nursey. There is fresh food in the fridge, eggs, milk, cheese and some other things in the kitchen. The gas is connected so you can make yourself something to eat or drink. If there is anything else you require please just press this buzzer,' and he indicated what looked like a door bell button on the inside of the caravan door.

'I'm going to have to lock you in I'm afraid but as I said before it is for your own safety.' The driver looked at her one last time as if to say, *'I'm only doing what I am told,'* and then closed the door. Nursey heard the sound of a padlock being attached and clicked shut so she knew she was not going anywhere.

The driver went back to the reception door and unlocked it, turning on the light as he went into the small office that used to be the reception area for the Hippodrome caravan park when it was still operational. But that was a few years ago now and the whole place felt a little damp and dusty, which of course it was. He slid off his beanie hat and took his phone out of his pocket. The screen said it was 05:35.

Early but not too early to inform Henri. He sent a short message to Henri which they had agreed to use once Nursey was safely out of the way. He checked his sent folder to make sure it had gone. *'The Hippo Has Landed,'* had reached its required destination.

All that Wally had to do now was while away a couple of days babysitting Nursey until he got word to bring her back. He had taken all the measures Henri had told him to and was certain they could not be traced.

.oOo.

Bertie Bedstead's meeting in Bristol had gone smoothly. He had met up with two of his old Army pals. They had both reached the rank of Major in the same regiment when Bertie was the Colonel. Bertie had been awaiting his coveted promotion to Brigadier at the time. They too had gone on to reach the rank of Colonel after Bertie had been promoted, but were now on rotation to the defence commercial arm as was often the way. He had gone through the contract with them and explained the advantages of the new style of bedding that would replace the current sheets and army blankets.

Their concerns about lack of discipline in making beds and the effect on morale were swiftly dealt with by Bertie, citing his own experience at the Ministry of Sleep and the beneficial effect the self-tucking duvets had on those who used them. Naturally he omitted to mention that Nursey was doing her level best to keep the traditional sheets and that he had more than a passing interest in the recommended supplier. After a pleasant lunch in the officers' mess (they retained a separate dining facility for military staff) Bertie had shaken hands and been reassured that the buying process could now be completed so that the formal orders would be placed within weeks.

He climbed into the official car they had laid on for him, complete with a rather pretty young Corporal to drive him. He gave her his most charming smile as she saluted him. The corporal remained impassive and just asked, 'To the station Sir?' before closing the rear door for him and getting into the driver's seat. They had been travelling only a couple of minutes when Bertie's phone rang.

'Bedstead speaking,' he said answering it without looking to see who the caller was.

'Good afternoon Director, it's Kurt here again. I'm sorry to bother you but I have an update on the situation with Nursey.'

'I hope it's good news Kurt,' replied Bertie, smiling at the Corporal's reflection in her rear-view mirror.

'I'm afraid not. Well not yet. You see, we thought we had found her because we picked up the GPS tracking signal from her phone but when we got to it, she had gone. The phone was in the caravan that was used to take her from the Ministry' continued Kurt.

Bertie made a mental note to give Henri an ear bashing for not doing something about the GPS when they had blocked her network signal.

'That's worrying Kurt, so where is she then?' Bertie tried to inject some concern and interest into his voice, as he knew from the text message sent to him earlier by Henri that Nursey was in the agreed secret location.

'We're not sure Director. The police are looking for her now and they have identified the car that took her away from the race course where the caravan was abandoned.'

'I thought that the case was being handled by that girl's father and we were working through him? You know the publicity would not be good for us,' hissed Bertie hoping the driver was not paying any attention.

'Police protocol means he has to hand the case over to someone else as Nursey is his sister. I believe a Detective Inspector Campbell is now in charge of the investigation but Nursey's brother is keeping us informed.'

'OK Kurt, thank you for updating me. Let's hope that Nursey is located soon. This is all very stressful. I should be back in about 2-3 hours so I will expect a full update then.' Bertie ended the call and looked out the window as they were getting close to the train station.

'Everything OK Sir?' enquired the corporal from the front seat. Bertie looked at her in the mirror again. So she had been listening. Things were not going well but he reflected that she did not have the context and was unlikely to gossip about a call she had overheard.

'Yes, fine, thank you corporal. Just a little staff issue back at my office. We're on top of it. Nothing to worry about.' He saw that the corporal nodded and smiled back at him. The car pulled up in front of the station and she got out to open the door for him, saluting once more.

'Thankyou Corporal, nice driving.' Bertie turned on the charm again.

'My pleasure Sir. Have a safe trip,' she replied and drove off.

A few minutes later Bertie's train arrived bang on time. He found his reserved seat in First Class and sat back in the deep leather chair, running through what he was going to say to Kurt when he got back to the Ministry. But first he had to deal with Henri – there had been one slip up already and that was one too many. At least the contract was signed now and the procurement team had assured him that the orders would be placed within weeks, although he knew from past experience that weeks in the defence systems could easily become months. He was in no rush.

His Caribbean island retreat would still be waiting for him.

Chapter 21

Buoyed by the news that the police had identified the Mitsubishi Shogun involved in taking Nursey, Felicity and Dougie went back into the main building of the Ministry in search of food. There was usually a side table in the dining room with snacks laid out such as scones, home-made cookies, fruit and various soft drinks (but not fizzy sugary ones, as Nursey had banned those).

Felicity and Dougie took a scone each and a glass of apple juice to a table by the window and swiftly ate their food as neither had consumed much for breakfast. Besides, Dougie was permanently hungry and always on the lookout for something to eat. Brad had quietly asked Felicity to make sure he didn't just eat chocolate or too many bags of crisps in an effort to maintain the sensible eating regime their mother had instigated from an early age.

'She's going to be OK, isn't she?' Dougie asked his sister as he stared at his empty plate.

'Of course she is. Dad's got it all under control and they've found the owner of the car so they should be able to track him down soon and we'll get Auntie Ange back,' Felicity reassured him. In the absence of their mother, Felicity always took the maternal role with Dougie. She knew she could never replace their mum, but Dougie needed someone to support and care for him when their Dad wasn't around.

She was completely confident that her father would be pulling all the strings he could behind the scenes.

At that moment, Kurt appeared and sat next to them.

'I've just found something you might be interested in,' he said, with a knowing look on his face. Immediately both children sat upright in their chairs looking at Kurt with wide eyes. Kurt looked around the room to make sure they were alone before he continued.

'You remember the work that was done by the company in Cheltenham to secretly install that device on our systems?' Felicity and Dougie nodded enthusiastically. 'Although I wasn't here when it was done, something about the name of the company seemed familiar. Well, you'll never guess what.' He left the sentence hanging for a moment.

'What is it – c'mon Kurt, tell us?' whispered Felicity also looking around the room. Dougie's eyes were alive with excitement and anticipation.

'The address that the car is registered to is the same address as the company who did the work. WSB. And the owner of the car is Walter Selwyn Braithwaite – WSB!' he exclaimed triumphantly.

'So that means the man who planted the device is the same man who kidnapped our aunt?' asked Dougie incredulously.

'Correct-o-mundo,' said Kurt, borrowing an English phrase he had heard the local staff use even though he wasn't quite sure what it meant.

Felicity and Dougie looked at each other for a second, both formulating the same question. Felicity asked it first.

'Why would he do that Kurt? Who else is he working with?'?'

'Those are very good questions young lady and ones to which we need answers.' Kurt replied, although he wasn't entirely sure that he knew how to get the answers. He need not have worried.

'Right, this is something that Horsey can definitely help us with,' said Felicity firmly. 'Horsey can communicate with the hippos and find out if they know anything. If we can find a connection, then we might understand why Nursey was taken. And why the music was swopped out.'

'How are you going to do that Felicity – would Horsey be willing to help us do you think?' asked Kurt.

'Oh yes, he quite liked Nursey when he met her so I'm sure he will help us out,' Felicity replied, nodding her head as she spoke to reinforce the message to Kurt. 'I just need to get my phone from Nursey's office and I can send him a Galloping Trot message on Trotter. It's OK Kurt, my Dad already asked me to contact Horsey and that phone is the only way to do it'

'Of course, why didn't I think of that?' asked Kurt smiling at Felicity as he knew this was something only she could have thought of. They all trooped back to Kurt's office and Kurt retrieved Felicity's phone from Nursey's office with his master key. Felicity tapped out the message to Horsey. All they could do now was wait.

.oОo.

Bertie arrived back at the Ministry and went straight to his office. He pulled his phone out and called Henri. To his surprise the ring tone was the French one, not the 'brrr-brrr' of the UK system, which meant Henri had returned to France.

'Henri, listen carefully' said Bertie once Henri had answered. 'Your man has been careless. The police have identified the car and traced the owner. It's only a matter of time before they find Nursey. And all of this happened because your man forgot about the GPS – he only blocked the calls. I thought he was an expert?'

'That's unfortunate Bertie, but it's not the end of the world,' cooed Henri, trying to calm his client, but internally furious that Wally had let him down – yet again.

'They only traced her as far as the race course as she left her phone in the caravan. Wally has taken her to a location they will never look and he stayed away from main roads so he would not be seen on cameras, so I'm confident that Nursey will remain out of the way until we decide to bring her back.'

'That's easy for you to say Henri, but I am the one who will be facing police questions. At some point, someone will leak this to the newspapers and television because they found your hippo recording as well,' replied Bertie angrily.

'By the time that happens we'll have returned Nursey. Don't worry Bertie, everything is under control. The worst thing you can do now is to panic, especially when we are so close. You did get the contracts to your contacts in procurement, didn't you?' Henri did his best to remain calm but inside he was calculating the odds and the steps he would need to take in case things didn't work out. At least he was safely back in France where British police could not question him. And once the contracts were placed, he would be the one making the profits – it was only their side agreement that benefitted Bertie. If it worked out that Bertie ended up in jail, it would be all the more for him. Henri allowed himself a small smile of satisfaction.

'Yes, the contracts are safe. I've held up my side of the bargain Henri. You need to hold up yours now,' snapped Bertie and terminated the call. He sat at his desk for a few moments, quietly fuming at the Frenchman's apparent lack of concern that they were potentially heading for a major problem. A problem that would land like a burning coal in Bertie's lap. He decided not to wait any longer and called Kurt.

'Kurt, Director Bedstead here,' he said brusquely when Kurt answered, 'any news on Nursey yet?'

'Nothing concrete Director' replied Kurt, 'but I have heard informally that the police have put out an 'APB' which I think means "All Points Bulletin" with the details of the car. Someone somewhere should spot the car and they can start to look for it. But at the moment, they don't know where it headed when it left the race course.'

'Let me know as soon as anything changes please Kurt. Naturally our concern is to have Nursey returned to us safely as quickly as possible.'

'Indeed it is Director – you will be the first to know,' Kurt assured him as he put down the phone. Somehow the Director's voice didn't reassure him. Kurt sensed that he was holding something back. If the Director was that concerned for a key staff member, why was he not speaking directly to the most senior police officer himself? Or to Felicity? He thought about it for a few moments and concluded that he could not figure out how the Director thought. Kurt focused instead on how he could help Felicity, whose concern, along with Dougie's, was obvious and sincere.

.oOo.

Felicity's phone buzzed with an incoming message. She grabbed it from Kurt's desk where it had been charging up and opened up the message. It was from Horsey! With a mixture of excitement and anxiety she opened it up and read it through. Kurt and Dougie were both staring intently at her for any sign of what it might contain. Felicity's brow furrowed.

'What is it? What does he say?' Dougie got his question in first. Felicity looked at him, then back to Kurt and back to Dougie again.

'I'm not 100% sure what it means. There is a lot of comment on Hippogram about the Hippopotamus Song and a recording made by the hippos who were in Rivertrot with Horsey. Apparently, you can buy it from 'Hippos-R-Us' and that some hippos regularly cross from France and then back again in cars towing caravans.'

'That's weird,' said Kurt looking even more puzzled. 'Why would hippos be in caravans to and from France? Is that even legal? Don't they have to be registered with something? Like a hippo chip?'

'I don't know either Kurt, but Horsey goes on to say that when they come to England they always take the caravans to the same site. It's called 'The Hippodrome' and he's not sure where it is but thinks it might be somewhere near the south coast.' Felicity read out Horsey's message with a degree of concern because she didn't understand what it really meant.

'We need to locate that caravan park. It would be an obvious place to take Nursey don't you think?'

'I need to call my Dad,' said Felicity. 'He can find it and rescue Nursey.'

'Yes, good plan. Let the police handle it from here,' agreed Kurt, feeling relieved that he would not be called upon for any heroics. He didn't do heroics – just careful, logical thinking.

'I'm still not sure why though,' mused Felicity, 'but I have an idea. There is someone else here who can help us.' Although she still felt nervous about her aunt, Felicity now had the same steely look of determination as Nursey.

There was no more hair twiddling.

Chapter 22

'That is brilliant Felicity. You really are a proper detective, aren't you?' Brad's voice was bursting with pride when his daughter called him with the update from Horsey Handbrake.

'First identifying the caravan, then the car and its tyres. You and Dougie have done great work. It's really helped the investigation. It won't take long for us to find Auntie Ange now.'

'We just want Auntie Ange to be safe and have her back as Nursey,' said Felicity quietly, still upset that her aunt had been taken at all. 'But the other stuff has been good fun as well – I like being a detective, although I'm not a proper one like you Dad. Well, not yet anyway.'

'You're off to a great start but there's a lot more to it. We'll talk about it another time. But for now, I must get this to the team on the case and then we have to figure out what is behind all of this. We need to catch the people responsible and get them locked up. I'll call you as soon as we have any more information. And Felicity ...' Brad left the question hanging in the air.

'Yes Dad?'

'I love you lots – and Dougie. And I'm VERY proud of you both,' said Brad and hung up before he got too emotional.

'*And I love you too Dad,*' thought Felicity.

Brad turned to Jock Campbell who was sitting right beside him and explained what Felicity had told him about the possible location and the name of the Hippodrome Caravan Park.

Jock rapidly typed some searches into his computer and found a number of hits for the name 'Hippodrome'. There was a lot about old music hall type cinemas and theatres that were now closed but he soon located the link for the caravan park and clicked on it. He quickly scanned the front page to make sure it was the right one and then selected 'map' from the menu. Sure enough, it was close to the South Coast near Bournemouth and as he zoomed in to the map he could read the street name and road number. Jock then dragged the 'Street' icon on to the road so he could see what it looked like.

The entrance to the park looked a little scruffy as if it had not been used in a while. He was able to make out and zoom into the sign saying, *'Hippodrome Caravan Park'* with the logo of the smiling hippo in blue polka dot pyjamas.

He motioned to Brad to take a look.

'I'm no expert on hippos but there is an obvious connection here – we just don't know what it is or if it is relevant yet.' said Brad

'Well Sir, no matter what it is, we need to get someone down there quickly. I'll put a call into Dorset HQ and see if they can get a couple of uniforms to take a look around for the Shogun. We can then have our guys on the way ready to back them up if it's a positive ID.' Jock had clearly got things under control. 'I'll tell the Super as well in case we need the chopper. They might be on the run for all we know Sir.'

'Good plan Jock' confirmed Brad, 'if you don't mind I'll stick around to see what happens, but you're running this one - OK?'

Jock nodded his agreement and picked up the phone to his counterpart in Dorset police to set the wheels in motion. They confirmed to him they had a car only ten minutes away that could drive by to check out the caravan park and report back. Jock looked at his senior officer and friend and gave him a reassuring smile. He could only imagine how Brad felt but as a professional he was not showing it.

Fifteen minutes later Jock's phone rang. It was Dorset.

'The uniforms have taken a look Jock and have confirmed there is a Silver Shogun matching the registration number you gave us parked next to what was the reception office. The park has been closed for a few years now so it looks pretty deserted otherwise,' came the voice of the Inspector Jock had spoken to.

'Was there any sign of the driver or anyone else?' he asked looking over at Brad.

'They can't be sure but they could see lights on in the reception office and a male figure inside again matching the description you gave us. They didn't see anyone else but they did report that there was a reasonably new caravan parked there that was the only one with a gas bottle – all the others were either static vans that clearly were not in use or others that were just sitting there.'

'That sounds promising,' replied Jock, 'did the person in the office spot your men?'

'They don't think so. They were very careful as per your instructions. What do you want us to do now?'

'Instruct them to stay out of sight and monitor the office and that other caravan as best they can. If the Shogun attempts to leave the park they should stop it and question the driver. I have a rapid response unit on its way now and they should be with you inside the hour. We may need extra back up so let me know the minute anything changes?'

Jock turned to Brad and looked him in the eye.

'I think this is our man, Sir. It is highly likely your sister is in that other caravan but I don't want to provoke a response until we have resources in place. I think that gives us the best chance of getting her unharmed – we don't know what this guy is up to so I don't want to take any unnecessary chances. But my instinct tells me he's just the messenger.' Jock was trying to reassure Brad but even though he was the officer in charge, he would change his plan if the DCI was not in agreement.

'That sounds reasonable Jock and you're right, we don't want to start something we can't finish and put Ange at risk. As long as nothing is happening then we're OK but the minute it changes, we should be ready to react,' said Brad partly in agreement and partly ensuring that Jock would take his views into account if needed.

'I'll ask Dorset to send a back-up now and keep it low key. I think they have heat sensitive scanners there so they might be able to detect if there really is someone inside the caravan – if not they can get them from the fire brigade.'

'Excellent idea Jock. Keep me posted – I'm just going to get something to eat.' Brad walked off to find the station canteen where he could sit and gather his thoughts.

.oOo.

Felicity had gone in search of Will along with Dougie. She didn't tell Dougie about Will's rather amusing business card but just that his dad worked for a big German company and that he was very good at finding out about companies on the internet.

They found him in the games room reading a book.

'Hi Will,' said Felicity breezily, 'haven't seen you for a while. What have you been up to?' Will looked up from his book and looked at Dougie inquisitively.

'This is my little brother, Dougie. Dougie, say hello to Will.' The two boys exchanged nods and smiles without making direct eye contact. It wasn't considered cool to actually shake hands when you're seven.

'Will, do you remember you said you knew how to find out about companies and stuff on the internet?' asked Felicity trying to sound casual.

'Yes of course, my father showed me how to do it,' replied Will, 'why, do you need someone to be investigated?'

'Actually, I do. You see, my aunt had to go away for a couple of days and there was someone trying to get hold of her and I only heard a little bit of the company name. I was wondering if you might be able to help me find it?'

'Should be no problem,' said Will confidently, 'but I don't have a computer. We had to hand them over when we got here.'

'Yes, so did we but I can get you access to one if you'll help me?' Felicity said giving him her sweetest smile.

'Ok' said Will, 'but how have you managed to get access to a computer?' he said looking a slightly suspicious.

'When I was a little bit ill earlier in the week, Nursey took me to see a doctor and she had to look up a few things to get consent or something. She introduced me to Kurt, who runs all the systems here and he said I could come back to him any time I needed something. I'm sure he'll help us if you could come to his office.'

Felicity was really winging it now and Dougie looked at her in amazement. He was impressed that his boring older sister was able to make things happen so easily. But he was smart enough to say nothing.

Kurt was in his office as usual and agreed, as he said he would, to let Will onto a screen with access to the internet. Felicity gave Will the information about WSB. Will started some searches in places Felicity had never come across before and within seconds he had a screen full of detailed information about WSB.

'That's the one,' said Felicity, glancing across at Kurt who was pretending not to listen.

'What does it mean about directors?' she asked, only a little innocently as this was precisely what she wanted.

'These are the people who basically run the company,' said Will. 'You can see that the Managing Director – he's the guy in charge mainly – is Walter Braithwaite of Cheltenham and that a non- executive director is Henri DuVay with an address somewhere in France, looks like the Loire Valley.'

'That's great Will, thanks – is there a phone number for the office?' Felicity asked trying to maintain her air of innocence. Will gave her the number.

'Actually, there is one more thing you could do for us Will. My dad always takes us to the same place for holidays and we, well that is, Dougie and me, were hoping to try somewhere else next year. Are there any other caravan and campsites we could look for?' Felicity turned to Dougie and gave him the merest hint of a smile that served as a warning to say nothing.

Will clicked on the mouse buttons and keyed in another search. Up came a list of caravan parks. There were hundreds of them all over the country.

'Did you want to look for somewhere specific?' asked Will, 'it would take ages to look at all of these.'

'South Coast maybe? Dad likes Dorset' said Felicity. Will typed some more and a shorter list came up but still a lot to consider. He slowly scrolled down the list until Felicity saw the one she wanted.

'Can you click on that one – it sounds nice,' she said and Will duly obliged by following the link to the Hippodrome Caravan Park.

'How do we know if it's any good or not?' she asked.

'Let's see what they say,' replied Will and clicked on a tab marked 'awards'. There, beaming back out at them, clutching some sort of framed certificate was a smiling, thin faced man with a long nose, standing next to the caravan park sign that clearly showed the hippo in the blue polka dot pyjamas.

The caption under the photo said, 'Hippodrome owner Walter Braithwaite with his Caravan Park of the Year award for Dorset 2010'.

'Well, that's a coincidence!' exclaimed Will. 'He's now the MD of WSB. I wonder what happened to the caravan park?' His curiosity was roused now as Felicity had guessed it would be. She felt sure there was a connection between WSB and the Hippodrome through the car. Now she had proof. Will started to type more and very quickly a similar screen of information to the one they had found about WSB came up. Under the section marked 'Directors' the same two names appeared. Walter Braithwaite and Henri DuVay.

Felicity and Dougie exchanged glances. They knew this meant that those two names were the ones behind their aunt's disappearance and the picture of the hippo was too much for it to be a coincidence. But they still didn't know what the reason was that Nursey had been taken. Felicity knew that they were close but something was eluding her. She didn't want to ask Will any more questions as she would either have to tell the most massive fib ever, or she would have to explain what was going on. She didn't feel it was right to tell the fib as she had already made up a story to get Will's help and she wasn't ready to tell him the real reason why just yet.

'That IS odd isn't it Will?' she said, looking at him. 'Maybe I will have to call Mr. Braithwaite to find out.'

'OK no problem,' said Will, but suspecting that there was more to this request that Felicity was letting on. He closed down the browser session and logged out.

'Why would this Mr. Braithwaite call here for your aunt though?' he asked with a slight, knowing, smile.

'She never said. I'll find out when she gets back,' replied Felicity, mentally crossing her fingers and hoping that Will would not ask any more questions. He didn't but she felt that he would like to. She glanced again at Dougie. He gave her a puzzled look in return that said, *"what are you up to?"*. They were on to something he didn't understand. He soon would.

Chapter 23

The unmarked black Octavia RS had made good time in the experienced hands of Constable Juan 'Speedy' Gonzalez, the Class 1 police driver assigned to take DC Kate O'Hara and Detective Sergeant Paul Harris for the rendezvous with the two officers from Dorset police. They were still parked up close by the Hippodrome caravan park where they could observe any movements without being noticed.

The PC in the passenger seat immediately clocked the unmarked car and got out to meet the new arrivals. He crouched by the front window of the Skoda and introduced himself as PC Tom Hardy and his colleague as PC Alan Brewster.

'No-one has come or gone since we arrived Sir,' he addressed himself to the Sergeant. 'What's the plan now?'

'Tom, we need you and PC Brewster to be ready to follow us in and block off any attempted escape. We have sufficient grounds to arrest this suspect, a Walter Selwyn Braithwaite of Cheltenham, on suspicion of abduction. There won't be a discussion – we're just going to nick him, once we've confirmed his identity. But we don't know how he might react so just keep your radios on and your eyes peeled in case he tries anything stupid' explained DS Harris.

'That sounds OK to me Sir. We'll be ready. We've checked that there is only one way in and out and this is it,' confirmed the local copper. 'And we've got back up on standby. Just in case.'

'Glad to hear that Tom but let's hope it isn't needed. Once we have secured the suspect we will search the caravan for the lady he's abducted. If she's OK we will take her back with us, but if not, we may need a medic to check her over.' Sergeant Harris looked at the local lad.

'Can you make sure there is one available?' he asked, to confirm this was understood and would be acted upon as required. It was.

'Right then, we'll make our move once you have briefed your driver – just give me the thumbs up when you're ready and follow us in.'

'Will do Sir,' replied PC Hardy and went back to join his partner. A few moments later he turned around to the black Octavia and gave the 'thumbs up' signal they were ready to go.

Speedy Gonzalez fired up the car's specially tuned engine and with a little more drama than was really necessary drove into the Hippodrome caravan park at speed and came to a sharp halt outside the door marked reception. DS O'Hara and Sergeant Harris were almost out of the car as it stopped and they rushed to the door, pushing it open and shouting 'Police, don't move,' as they crashed into the office.

Wally Braithwaite literally fell off his chair as he was woken from his doze by the sound of the police officers suddenly appearing in front of him. The Sergeant spoke to him first.

'Walter Braithwaite?' he asked. Wally nodded as his mouth didn't seem to be working. This was not part of the plan he had signed up to.

'I am Detective Sergeant Paul Harris of Severn Valley Police and this is DC Kate O'Hara. I am arresting you on suspicion of abducting

Angelina Twissleton-Smythe, also known as Nursey Corners, from the Joshua Turner Institute yesterday between the hours of 10pm and 10.30pm.'

Wally continued to make no sound – he couldn't really comprehend what was going on. This wasn't supposed to be possible. The police continued to read him his rights and he was aware of being handcuffed by the younger woman.

'Kate, you stay here and watch Mr Braithwaite. I'll see where Nursey is.'

'Sarge,' she acknowledged.

DS Harris looked at Wally with contempt. 'Don't try anything just because you think you can overpower a woman. DC O'Hara here is a black belt in mixed martial arts. And there are two other large coppers outside to help her. Just in case you had any smart ideas.'

He stepped quickly outside the office and looked around to see the newer caravan – the same make as the one in the description he had been given – standing about 20 metres away. He ran to the door and saw it was padlocked from the outside. He banged on the door and called out 'Police – is there anyone in there?'

'Yes, I am in here' called Nursey. 'Please let me out,' she said with considerable calmness considering her ordeal.

'Are you Angelina?' asked DS Harris.

'Yes I am,' confirmed Nursey.

'This is DS Paul Harris, Severn Valley Police ma'am. I'll be back in a moment with something to break this padlock. You're safe now,' he said.

DS Harris went back to the office and looked at Wally. 'Key for the padlocked caravan – where is it?' he demanded. This was no time for pleasantries. Wally nodded towards the drawer in the desk which Harris pulled open to reveal the Yale padlock key. He grabbed it and ran back to the caravan, unlocked the door and saw a rather startled but relieved Nursey standing inside.

'Are you OK ma'am,' he asked again, 'you've had quite an ordeal? We can get you a doctor if you need one.'

'I'm an ex-Army nurse, Detective Sergeant Harris. I've had worse nights than being driven around the country. At least nobody was shooting at me.' Nursey smiled at him.

'But I'd love a cup of tea. And thank you, I wasn't looking forward to the rest of my holiday here,' she said with a wry smile.

'It's not me you need to thank ma'am,' he said, 'it was your niece who worked out where you were and your nephew who identified the car so we could trace the owner. Without their help, this could have worked out very differently.'

'They are very special kids for sure and I am looking forward to seeing them,' said Nursey with a wave of relief washing over her.

'Let's get you back to the local nick with the boys from Dorset and we can sort you out a cup of tea and then get you back home,' said DS Harris, smiling with relief as well.

DC O'Hara guided Wally into the back of the Dorset car and Paul Harris made way for Nursey to take the front seat of the Octavia and they followed the white Mondeo to the local police station, with their blue lights flashing to keep traffic at bay. On the way, Paul Harris called Jock Campbell to tell him the good news, which he could hear Jock relaying immediately to DCI Frampton sitting next to him.

'The DCI says well done lads. And thank you. We'll get a full debrief when you get here,' said Jock with a huge smile on his face.

Wally was taken to Dorset HQ and charged there. He would be transferred back to Severn Valley later that day once the paperwork had been completed. Nursey got her cup of tea and sat happily chatting to her rescuers, all of whom spoke very highly of her brother, the DCI. She knew he was good as his job but it was a little embarrassing to hear such praise directly. It was not in Nursey's nature, nor her brother's, to be comfortable in the limelight.

.oOo.

Brad had immediately called Felicity and Dougie at the Ministry to break the good news and they spontaneously cheered out loud in Kurt's office when the call came in. Everyone was thrilled that Nursey would soon be back. But Felicity knew that this was not the end. They still did not know why this had happened and who else might be involved beyond Wally Braithwaite. There was a connection to Henri DuVay through the companies they both owned but she didn't yet know what that had to do with Nursey being abducted.

'We should go and see the Director to tell him the good news,' Kurt turned to Felicity and Dougie.

'Yes, we should. I'm sure he would want to know,' agreed Felicity, although like Kurt, she still had a sense of unease about Bertie Bedstead from the first time she saw him on the night she arrived.

Kurt called Bertie in his office and said they had some news to share. Bertie told them to come over at once. 'Well, this is excellent news all round,' he beamed at Kurt, Felicity and Dougie. 'What a relief eh?'

'Yes Director, of course. We are all pleased that Nursey has been found and will soon be back with us,' said Kurt smiling.

'But we don't know why this happened Kurt,' interjected Felicity. 'Why would anyone want to take Nursey away in the first place?' She glanced over at the Director and saw a tiny hint of a smirk cross his lips.

'I'm sure the police will get to the bottom of this. Your father's a detective I hear,' he directed the question to Felicity.

'Yes, he is, but he wasn't allowed to work on this case. Police rules.' stated Felicity still scrutinising the Director whose eyes would not maintain contact with her. He looked distinctly uncomfortable and shot a quick glance in the direction of the picture on his wall.

Felicity spotted him doing it and waited until he was looking the other way at Kurt to sneak a peek at it herself. It was a photo of the Director standing next to a sign with a small logo on it. It was a hippo. In blue polka dot pyjamas. And there was another man at the edge of the photo leaning against the other end of the sign. She couldn't read all of the wording but it looked like 'Belle Vue'. That would be enough for Will to go on. She felt sure that this could be the missing link.

'Right then, when Nursey gets back, we'll have a little celebration shall we? Only right and proper. I'll see to it so let me know when she arrives,' boomed Bertie, back to his parade ground best.

Chapter 24

With Wally in the custody of Dorset police and his sister safely installed in the back of an unmarked car now heading towards his own station, Brad Frampton was feeling good – a heady mixture of relief, pride and anticipation. So much had happened since the last day of their holiday that it felt like months had passed but it was only a few days. Although they had apprehended one of the people involved in taking his sister Brad knew that there was still some detective work to be done to uncover who was behind it.

His initial impression was that Wally was not the brains of the operation. He was just following instructions from someone else and whilst he would pay a heavy price for his role in the crime, it was the people who had instigated it that Brad really wanted.

He needed to speak to Nursey to gather as much information as possible about her ordeal as she was the only one who could tell them exactly what had happened. The information that his son and daughter had uncovered was also crucial in establishing links between Wally and this shady character, Henri DuVay. Even the background picture they had built up from Horsey Handbrake's input after he had looked on Hippogram had been vitally important. No clue was too small – the answer was always in the little details that often were missed or dismissed early on in investigations as not being relevant. In Brad's experience, everything was relevant until proven otherwise.

His phone buzzed. It was the desk Sergeant, Bill Hurst.

'Your sister has just arrived Sir. I thought you'd like to know,' said Bill, ever the master of understatement.

'Thanks Bill, I'll come down now,' replied Brad, as jumped up from his desk to meet Ange who had been shown into an interview room. They were joined by Jock Campbell as he would be the one to de-brief Ange – Brad could only be an observer. Kate brought in cups of tea and sat with the other two officers and Ange as they started to go over everything that had happened since she first became suspicious that something odd was happening to the children on the sleep-walking programme.

Everything she told them matched exactly with what they had observed or knew already and Ange wasn't really able to provide more detail on Wally as he had said so little.

'There was one thing that I thought a bit weird though,' she said as she tried to recall every little detail, knowing the way her brother's mind worked. 'I checked the duvets on the beds in the caravan and the label said, 'Made in France, DuVay Duvets'. She looked at Brad as he had sat up as if he had been startled.

'DuVay? Are you sure Ange?' he said. Brad looked at Jock and Kate who were also aware of the connection that Felicity had uncovered with Will's help.

'Yes of course. I thought it was a little joke – you know, *DuVay Duvets*? Why, is there something significant in that name?' she asked her own curiosity also aroused now.

'It could be,' interjected Jock, anxious to regain control of the interview, 'we think there is a connection between Wally Braithwaite, the guy who drove you, and a *"Henri DuVay"* as they have both been

directors of the Wally's company WSB and the Hippodrome caravan park they took you to. It was your niece who found that out.'

'WSB also did work at the Ministry. I'm sure of it,' Ange said, still trying to make sense of these apparently random connections. 'When we found the black box that had been installed on the computer systems, the work had been done by WSB. And it was done when Kurt, our technical manager, was on holiday. So, that can only mean it was authorised by Bertie.'

All three detectives looked at each other and back to Ange. This was getting more serious as it started to look as if the Director of the Turner Institute might be involved as well, or at least been aware of something untoward. But all they had was circumstantial evidence that would not stand scrutiny. They needed more proof but for now they at least had a new line of enquiry.

.oOo.

Felicity was worried that Will would be suspicious if she asked him again to check something on a weak pretence. He was a smart kid and seemed to be able to sense when something wasn't quite right. He obviously had his grandfather's head for business. She decided that she had to take the risk of telling him what had happened and that he would keep it quiet until the full truth had emerged. `Well,' she thought, `if his father trusts him to analyse all these business questions then he's probably used to keeping a secret.' Besides, if she tried to charm him again and he refused, then she was stuck. Felicity found him in his favourite seat by the window in the games room and sat down beside him.

'Will, I need your help again. And if I tell you why, you have to promise me you won't tell anyone, not even your dad.' Felicity was both insistent and pleading. She knew he would be hooked by the secrecy – every kid liked secrets.

'Well, of course I will keep it secret Felicity – as long as I know what it is you need me to do,' countered Will.

'You can do it – it's similar to the last thing but this time we need to look in France.' she said mysteriously.

'In France?' Will's eyebrows shot up along with his voice. 'Now that sounds much more interesting. Our company has loads of stores in France and I have visited some of them when we were on holidays. What do I need to find out for you?'

They walked back to Kurt's office where Felicity had again requested access to a computer from Kurt, who, knowing that it was important to help find the people who had taken Nursey, readily agreed. Will searched for the 'Belle Vue'. Several came up but one stood out. It was the Belle Vue caravan park and it was in the Loire Valley.

Felicity immediately recognised the same sign and, crucially, the logo with the smiling hippo.

'Can you find out who the owners are Will?' Felicity asked. Will's fingers flew over the keyboard and he focused intently on the screen, scrolling down though a lot of search results in French. He glanced over at Felicity.

'It's OK, I can speak French as well,' he smiled at her. *Of course he could*, she thought – most Europeans could manage two or three languages by the time they went to senior school.

'Aha – here it is,' he exclaimed. Felicity leaned forward with excitement but also nervous that her hunch would prove to be wrong.

'Main shareholder is Henri DuVay and he is also a director,' he read out aloud, looking at Felicity sensing that this was not a coincidence. There's a picture of him. Felicity leaned forward to see a slightly older version of the person in the photo hanging in the Director's office.

'And also listed is, Bertrand Alexander Carrington, with an address in England,' said Will.

'Yes!!!' cried Felicity, loudly enough to bring Kurt out from his machine room to see what had happened. 'That's it. That's the Director's real name. He must know Henri DuVay and Henri must know Wally Braithwaite. And with the work done here by WSB we are sure the Director knows Braithwaite.'

'So why is this significant,' asked Will, 'I'm not sure I understand.'

'Nor do I yet Will, but we can figure this out once I speak to my aunt,' replied Felicity. She will be here soon for the celebration so we'll go over this before we meet the Director.'

Felicity called her father to arrange a meeting with him, Nursey and of course Dougie, before they all went to see Bedstead. She was so close but one or two bits of key information eluded her – with those in place, she felt sure it would all finally make sense. But first there was one more question for Horsey.

Chapter 25

Brad arrived at the Ministry with Nursey in his own car – it was technically still his day off so he was not using an official police car. He pressed the intercom buzzer at the gate and they opened at once. Kurt was expecting them of course.

They all met up in Nursey's office – Kurt, Brad, Nursey Felicity and Dougie. There was much hugging and cracking of jokes but everyone was relieved to have Nursey back safely. They had about half an hour before they were due to meet the Director in his office where he had promised a champagne toast. However, they all knew that somehow they needed to deal with the strong possibility that the Director himself had been involved in Nursey's abduction.

Brad explained all the evidence they had accumulated and brought in some new information that had been uncovered since Nursey was released from the caravan at the Hippodrome. Dorset police had been very thorough and had searched the site after Wally was driven away. They had found large quantities of newly packaged DuVay duvets in the mobile caravans that were parked at the site. From the descriptions given Nursey was certain they were the same type as she had seen – namely the 'self- tucking' variety.

Armed with that knowledge Nursey had contacted her husband who was still well connected in the military and asked him to speak to his contacts on the Army's commercial side. She had always been a little suspicious of Bertie and his rather self-important comments about his career in the armed forces so was not too surprised to find that he wasn't quite what he seemed. Her husband had managed to establish that the top Army brass were reviewing use of bedding and there was a move towards duvets and away from traditional sheets and blankets. Bertie's name had come into the conversation as they were expecting an endorsement from him for a new style of duvet.

Felicity's phone message to Horsey had turned up that the main base for the hippos in France was the Belle Vue so there did seem to be a connection between use of the Hippopotamus Song, the music, the sleep-walking and the transport of duvets in caravans.

All of this was of course just conjecture at this stage – they needed to confront the Director and get him to confess. So, when they came to meet him their plan was worked out.

.oOo.

'Do come in my dear Nursey,' the director honked at them. 'How marvellous to have you back. What an ordeal eh? You are OK, aren't you?' His concern was very loud and seemed a little contrived as Nursey, Kurt, Felicity and Dougie went into the big office.

'It was a little trying at times Bertie,' Nursey said with a bit of a sigh, 'but thanks to the efforts of Kurt, Felicity and young Dougie here, they managed to track me down and the police did the rest. It's certainly not something I would wish to repeat.'

'Indeed not Nursey. I would not wish that on anyone, not even my worst enemy,' proclaimed the Director.

Felicity looked across at Nursey and saw her imperceptible nod. This was her cue.

'That's not strictly true, is it Director?' said Felicity speaking softly.

Bertie looked startled and his face flushed. He managed to keep his composure and fixed his gaze on Felicity.

'I'm sure I don't know what you mean young lady,' he said, 'Nursey is one of our most valued members of staff and I have known her for many years. Why on earth would I wish any harm on her?' He spoke with a slight menace in his voice but was conscious not to be seen to bully a child.

'We know about your proposed contract with the Army to supply self-tucking duvets from Henri DuVay. We know that DuVay set up the music to change the way the sleep-walking programme worked to get the children out of bed and into your caravan, so that DuVay's duvets were preferred over sheets and blankets. We know that DuVay instructed Wally Braithwaite to get Nursey out of the way once she had discovered the music swop and we know that YOU authorised the installation of a device to enable that to happen.' Felicity fixed the Director with a steely stare and waited for his response.

Bertie was started to turn even redder but he managed to keep calm and not raise his voice.

'I have no idea what you are talking about Felicity. I know you are upset about your aunt being taken – we all are – but what you are suggesting is preposterous. I don't even know Henri DuVay or Wally Braithwaite.'

'Perhaps then you can explain why Henri DuVay appears in that photograph with you that is on the wall behind you?' asked Felicity not shifting her gaze from the Director.

'That's someone else. I've never heard of this Henri DuVay,' he stuttered.

'So, if you have never heard of Henri DuVay then why are you and he co-owners and directors of the Belle Vue caravan park that is in the picture? Seems to be a strange coincidence, doesn't it Mr. *Carrington*?' continued Felicity, emphasising the last name to let Bertie know she knew who he really was. But before Bertie had a chance to reply she went on.

'If you have never heard of Wally Braithwaite how did your signature get on the order to his company to install this spy kit?' she said, producing a copy of the order and slapping it on his desk.

'It also seems odd that Henri DuVay, the man you say you don't know is also a co-director of WSB, the company you paid to put a black box into your own systems, doesn't it?' Felicity was on a roll now and was not going to let up.

'And I suppose you are going to tell us that it is just a coincidence that there are caravans full of these duvets, the same ones that were in the caravan used to take Nursey away, in a caravan park in Dorset, also owned by Braithwaite and DuVay?'

Bertie was spluttering now and had gone from being flushed to all the colour draining from his face which was starting to bead with sweat.

'Well, er, um, I, er, well, just because you've found all this information it doesn't mean to say I was involved in any way. You can't prove it. I already told you, I would not wish to harm Nursey. This is ridiculous!' he puffed, starting to shift uncomfortably in his seat.

'That might be the case Director if you had not gone to the Bristol this morning with contracts endorsed by you to place large orders for self-tucking duvets from DuVay Duvets in France. A contract from which you and Monsieur DuVay would no doubt stand to make a lot of money!!'

There was a stunned silence in the room. Even though Kurt, Nursey and Dougie knew all of this and what Felicity had planned to say to the Director, it was still a shock to hear it all out in the open.

They all stared at Bertie, waiting for him to respond. He mopped his brow with a handkerchief and took a few deep breaths, looking at each of them in turn. A sly little smile crossed his lips.

'OK then Miss Detective, what are you going to do as you have no proof of any of this? You can't arrest me, can you?' he barked at her, with a triumphant look on his face.

'No, she can't,' Brad's voice came from the now open door. 'But I can.'

Bertie's face froze and his mouth was suspended in a look of utter surprise as he turned to see Brad, flanked by two large uniformed police officers.

'DCI Brad Frampton. Severn Valley Police. I am arresting you on suspicion of aiding and abetting a kidnap, and suspicion of intent to commit fraud. I'm sure we'll come up with a few more in the fullness of time Mr. Bedstead but that's plenty be going on with and to get you 5-10 years behind bars.'

Bertie looked around the room to the smiling faces of everyone else. He knew the game was up but he wasn't going to let them see it.

'You can't do this. You have no evidence,' he spluttered.

'Oh yes, we can and oh yes we do,' retorted Brad, and turning to the two uniformed officers who had helped him at the race course, said 'PC Davidson, arrest that man.'

As the two coppers moved to handcuff Bertie and read him his rights, he started to move away from them.

'I wouldn't advise that Sir. You don't want to be adding resisting arrest to the charge sheet now do you?' Brad said pointedly to Bertie.

'PC Davidson here has been chasing caravans this morning and I'm sure he won't have any difficulty in arresting you.'

Bertie was led out of his office and into the back of the waiting police car which then sped off back to the station.

Brad came over to his sister and his children and hugged them all, and shook hands warmly with Kurt.

'Now, where's that champagne? I heard there was a celebration going on!'

Epilogue

After all the excitement of cornering Bertie Bedstead with the evidence they had accumulated and seeing him carted off by the police, they all sat down and there was a feeling of great relief that settled over everyone. It had all turned out well in the end but it could so easily have been different.

The help they had from Horsey Handbrake, the unexpected discovery of the altered music leading to the hippos and the discovery of the installation of the snooping device by Wally had a major impact on rescuing Nursey so quickly.

Nursey still could not really believe that Horsey was able to do all those amazing things – dancing, talking, communicating with hippos. Kurt was irritated that his secure systems had been breached but he consoled himself with the fact it had been done by his own boss whilst he was on holiday.

Felicity had made some new friends and before they left she sought out Gail and Mandy to explain that she was leaving the Ministry early as she needed to look after her brother. They too all hugged and promised to keep in touch.

Will.E.Widl was finally cured of his bed wetting and was allowed to go on holiday with his parents back to Germany. He had kept his promise not to tell anyone about his role in finding the links between the various people involved in taking Nursey. He had invited Felicity to come and see them in the Black Forest but Felicity didn't think her dad would be so keen.

With the Director gone, the American owners of the Institute needed to replace him urgently and had approached Nursey to take over the role, which she was happy to accept as it meant she could finally run things the way she wanted although she was getting used to the idea that maybe duvets weren't so bad after all – just not French ones as Henri DuVay was still at large in France.

The hippos from Rivertrot were reunited at the race course and managed to land a small part in Horsey's new production which allowed them to show off their legendary dancing skills. They had all ordered new blue polka dot pyjamas from Hippos-R-Us.

Brad took Felicity and Dougie home to their own beds and they had a nice family meal together – Brad cooked their favourite shepherd's pie – and they spend the evening telling and re-telling all the twists and turns of their adventures of the past few days. They all agreed it was time to try a new place for holidays next year as they had had enough of caravans for now.

Darkness fell and Brad started the bedtime regime they had kept to since their mum passed away. Once they were both in bed with lights out, Brad sat in the kitchen and poured himself a large whiskey. He was certain his daughter would not give up on her dream of becoming a detective and deep down he was confident she would be a very good one. Dougie, well, Dougie was still a little boy and no doubt next week he'd want to be a footballer again. Either way, he was intensely proud of them and knew their mother would be too.

Upstairs Felicity lay in her bed, listening to the silence interrupted only by the occasional owl. As she was drifting off to sleep, she was vaguely aware of a faint rhythmic humming sound. She listened intently. The tune was familiar and she felt herself mouthing the words 'Mud, mud, glorious mud'. It could only mean one thing.

The hippos were on the move again. She sensed that they would somehow play a part in her life in the near future. But until then, there was school on Monday to deal with.

If you want a taster for the next Felicity Frampton Mystery
See the Prologue to the next book here

Horsey Handbrake and the
Missing Silk Pyjamas

Horsey Handbrake and the Missing Silk Pyjamas

Prologue

`Ladies and Gentlemen, boarding will commence in 15 minutes. Please return to your vehicles. Thank you and we wish you a pleasant crossing.' The disembodied voice boomed out over the speakers.

Felicity Frampton gently kicked her dad's leg under the table of the waiting area at the spanking new ferry terminal in Portsmouth. He had been lost in his own thoughts and the far-away look in his eyes told her he had been thinking about her mum. She had always organised the holidays when she was alive. She was the one who spoke fluent French. And now her dad was heading to France with barely a handful of words of the language and full responsibility for two kids. Felicity knew he would be a bit nervous and apprehensive but equally would be determined not to let it show.

`Come on Dad, let's get going!' she exclaimed excitedly as there was a sudden surge in people all heading out of the café and heading purposefully to the lines of cars outside. She grabbed her backpack at the same time as her brother Dougie got up. He was even more excited to be going on the ferry to France. At last their badgering had paid off and their father had given in to the idea of a holiday abroad.

Brad Frampton took one more look around the table to make sure they had left nothing behind.

`Right then you two — final check' he said brightly, secretly as excited as his children.

`Passports?'

`Yes' came the simultaneous reply as both Felicity and Dougie waved their passports under his nose for about the tenth time that morning.

`Euros?'

They brandished the small wallets they had both been given with €30 in cash that they could spend on their own.

`Ferry ticket?'

`You've got that Dad' sighed Felicity as Dougie rolled his eyes.

`Oh yeah, so I do` replied Brad, laughing, knowing full well he did. `Nothing stopping us now. France here we come!'

It was a tight squeeze getting all of their gear into their small family car and with Felicity sitting in the passenger seat, Dougie was barely visible in the back beside all the luggage next to him on the folded down bit of the back seat. But he didn't mind – he was in control of the snacks and drinks.

The cars in front of them started to move so Brad started the engine and they followed the line into the cavernous interior of the ferry. Dougie had told them all about it – they had decided to take the fast crossing so they were on the Australian built catamaran. This made the chances of a rough crossing, and therefore feeling seasick, much less. Plus, it was only three hours, so they wouldn't get too bored.

Brad had also splashed out on Club Class seats for the outward journey as he wanted to get their first French holiday off to a really good start. He knew that if his kids were happy then they would all have a much better time. That meant keeping them well fed, especially Dougie, and making sure they could have time to do things on their own as well as together. He really hoped they would make new friends at the caravan and camp site he had booked. It looked as if it had superb facilities and was popular with other nationalities, especially the Dutch, who were always friendly and easygoing.

Once the car was secured they made their way up the stairs to the fully enclosed decks and found their large comfy reclining seats in the Club lounge – this too was a surprise treat for them.

`Wow this is amazing Dad' cried Dougie. He had only ever seen pictures of the ferry and now he was on it. He could hardly believe his luck.

`Are these our seats all the way over?' asked Felicity, her eyes wide open and a huge smile on her face.

`I think so' said Brad with a twinkle in his eye, `there won't be anyone else getting on half way across'

`Oh dad, that's a terrible joke' they groaned, but laughed all the same.

Once they were settled in their seats, they walked to the front looking straight out so they could see where they were going. Felicity and Dougie then set about exploring the rest of the ship and quickly found the restaurants, the various TV screens showing the latest films and the small but well stocked tax-free shop with all manner of French things they had never seen before. Felicity and Dougie came running back to Brad, breathless and flushed with excitement.

`You should see this ship dad – it's wicked' said Dougie, his eyes still like saucers and incredulous.

`When you stand on the open deck at the back the jets of water from the engines are HUGE!' he exclaimed.

`I'll take a look shortly' replied Brad, `and then we can get something to eat. I'm starving – are you two hungry?'

The question was superfluous – they were always hungry – but they both nodded enthusiastically anyway. The complimentary breakfast of a croissant or pain au chocolat had barely touched the sides.

With their excellent but reasonably priced meal and exploring the entertainment on-board, as well as reading their books and gawping out of the windows, the time passed really quickly and very soon they were docking in Cherbourg. As they drove off the huge ferry there were lots of reminders to "Tenez a Droite/Drive on the right" and Brad took things fairly easily until he was accustomed to driving on the "wrong side". It came to him more easily than he had thought at first and soon the roads were almost empty of traffic and they could zip along at their own pace. Brad marvelled at the super smooth road surfaces on the A28 as they headed south past Alencon ("ooh-er, twinned with Basingstoke" they all chimed together when they saw the sign) and towards Le Mans.

Being a policeman, Brad was all too aware of the need to stay within the speed limits and be vigilant for any other traffic rules that differed from home. He didn't think his British warrant card would cut much slack with an over- zealous Gendarme and decided not to put it to the test.

`Dad' said Felicity with that enquiring tone he recognised, that meant the question which followed would not have a simple yes or no answer. It rarely was with his daughter, who had worked out that asking him directly was not the best way to get what she wanted.

`Yes, my precious' replied Brad, not talking his eyes off the road, `what is it?'

`Will our phones work in France?

`They should do Felicity but you know they are only really for emergencies or for texting each other if we get separated?' Brad tried not to sound too stern as normally Felicity and Dougie were both very responsible with phones but he sensed there was another reason.

`Can I turn mine on to see if it does?' came the question.

`Let's wait until we stop, eh?' suggested Brad. `That way we can all check and see what has happened.' The last thing he wanted was Dougie and Felicity shouting out questions about their phones that he could only answer by looking. If they were stopped, he could answer them all at once.

`OK – I need to use the loo anyway' replied Felicity and Dougie said he did too.

`There is a service station in about 10 kilometres. We can try that? Should be no more than 10 minutes.' Brad could see Dougie nodding in the rear-view mirror and he shot a glance across to Felicity to see her do the same.

At the "Aire" which was operated by Total, they managed to sit outside in the warm sunshine after Brad had waited for Felicity to emerge from the "toilettes". He had asked another British lady if she could just ensure Felicity was OK once inside and she readily agreed. She had her own two kids with her and her husband stayed outside with their son.

`First time in France' asked the man looking at Brad.

`Yeah, afraid so – but it seems OK so far' Brad said lightly

`It's fine as long as you don't worry too much about French drivers' he laughed. `We've been coming for years and we've had no problems really – you just have to let them do things their way.'

`I'll bear that in mind – good advice' chuckled Brad, starting to relax.

Once everyone was finished they sat down again and turned on all three phones. After a moment or two they all got successive "pings" as text messages arrived to welcome them and advise how much calls would cost to make and receive.

`Well, that's good` beamed Brad looking at each one in turn, ` we're all on the same network. Let's hope the signal is better here than at home.'

As he said that Felicity's phone pinged again.

`Oh, looks like I have a message Dad. Is it OK to read it?' she asked, sticking with the advice her father had given her many times.

`OK – go for it' confirmed Brad, `I'm sure you don't have a French boyfriend yet' he laughed. Felicity just sighed and shook her head as she read through the message. She was silent for about a minute.

'Well, what's it about then' teased Brad, 'Dougie's dying to know who it's from. Aren't you Dougie?'

Felicity looked up at her father and then to her brother, as if deciding who to address.

'It's from Horsey. He's in France too. A place called Deauville. It's in Normandy apparently, very up-market. He says he is putting on a new show here with some French horses.'

'That's nice. Good that he keeps in touch with you after all that mystery at the Ministry with Auntie Ange.' Brad was relieved that it wasn't anything more sinister. He was used now to the idea that Felicity's Irish dancing teacher was a horse – a talking one at that, and quite the character.

'There's more dad. He says he wants my help. It says something about hippos and silk pyjamas going missing. It's hard to be sure as it has come from Trotter and sometimes it doesn't translate very well' said Felicity looking puzzled. She could just imagine Horsey using the special keyboard he had designed for horses' hooves so they could put messages into their own Trotter system.

'That *is* strange' agreed Brad, 'why would he be telling you that?'

'He says the hippos should be in the Loire valley – that's where we're going isn't it?' asked Felicity, remembering the picture of the hippos at the Belle Vue park that had been the key to getting Bertie Bedstead arrested.

'That's right, we are – how would Horsey know that though?' retorted Brad, trying not to go into full detective mode.

'I told him we were going to France this year so I mentioned the Loire Valley when he asked where – just in case we wanted to come and see his show.' Felicity looked at her father expecting to be told off but he wasn't upset – Brad knew how fond Felicity was of Horsey and the whole DuVay duvet case had only strengthened their friendship. He was slightly irritated that they had not been able to arrest Henri

DuVay, the accomplice to Bedstead, as he had disappeared back to France.

`He says he will be in touch soon once he knows more.' Felicity frowned not really sure what this meant.

`OK then, let's wait until anything else comes through. There should be wi-fi where we're going and we can get messages on my laptop if we need to.' Brad looked at them both. Dougie was trying not to appear interested but Brad sensed he was getting quite excited at the prospect of another mystery to be solved.

Felicity was pensive. Of course she wanted to help Horsey but she also wanted a "normal" holiday and knew that her dad was keen to have some time to relax and unwind from the daily pressures of being a senior detective.

`Yeah, we'll do that. Is it OK if I just text Horsey to let him know we're here?' she asked gently. Brad nodded.

`Right, that's settled. Time to hit the road again if we are to get to Amboise in time for dinner` declared Brad. `Shall we play "Stobart Snap" but with French lorries? Let's see how many Norbert Dentrassangle trucks we can spot!'

They all piled back into the car and opened the windows to cool it down. It was nice to have warm air and sunshine. But it was the prospect of another mystery that was the hottest topic.

For more information about Horsey Handbrake
please visit the author's FaceBook page at:
https://www.facebook.com/glenn.coe.108

and/or visit the Handbrake Publishing website:
www.handbrakepublishing.co.uk

A conversation with author Glenn Coe

Your background is in business. How did you get into writing? Have you always written?

Writing is a core skill in all types of commercial activity – if you cannot communicate in writing then it creates all kinds of problems. Lots of people said they liked my "style" and several also said "you should write a book". But, as I frequently pointed out, there is a massive difference between the occasional humorous email and creating a novel.

In a sense therefore, yes, I have always written and have always enjoyed the written word, but I never thought I would make the transition to writing a book of any kind or writing just for the pleasure of writing.

Retiring from the pressures of the corporate world after 40 years finally gave me the time and the head space to think about actually creating something original. It took a while to take shape, but once I started, it was fine.

How do you write? Are you a plotter or a starter (as in just get on with it)?

I'm a bit of both. I did a short overview of the story and the characters first – after the initial "aha!" moment in my head. For Nursey Corners, I then took it in stages but found that actually writing the chapters and bringing the characters to life on the page, changed the way the story developed.

At times, I had to write my way out of a blockage until the way forward became clearer. By about the half way mark, I knew the finishing line and then drove the story towards that conclusion. I kept going back over it to ensure it all made sense which also helped come up with interesting side stories and inject some pace into the adventure.

Many of your characters have funny names – how did you come up with them?

Nursey is a typical example. One day, whilst making the bed, my partner Liz asked me why I was taking so long. I replied it was because I wanted to tuck the sheets in properly, the way they do in hospitals. She told me to hurry up as there wasn't time for my "Nursey Corners" and the name then became this imaginary character. The other main ones happened in similar ways – Felicity, Horsey, Bertie Bedstead and the hippos as examples. The challenge then was to devise a story line that allowed them to come to life. That's when the idea of a mystery with a child detective came to me.

What other authors inspire you?

I read a wide range of other novels, as well as non-fiction. I love the dry humour of Bill Bryson and his insightful observations. This may seem odd, but I don't read other books for children and that is quite deliberate. I wanted to create my own style and not end up subconsciously copying someone else. It was also important to me that the stories espoused the values I believe in, of which many are sadly disappearing. That's why, for example, Felicity and Dougie are not fashion or gadget obsessed.

Your book has some stylish illustrations – how did you come up with those?

Actually, I didn't. They are the work of my son, who is a talented artist and animator. I gave him the story, explained what I thought the characters might look like but left it totally to him. They are also, like the descriptions in the book, a little light on detail. Again, this is deliberate – I wanted to leave as much as possible to the reader's imagination.

A lot of the humour in the book is quite subtle – do you think children will laugh?

I have tried to make this book work on two levels. There is a level of humour that a 9 year-old might tune into and then there is stuff that is aimed more at adults. I did it this way as I really want parents to read the book to their own children as well as kids reading it for themselves. If the parents get a giggle from a reference that the kids don't, they might be more inclined to read it out loud. That way it encourages both parents and children to read more. I love the Wallace and Gromit stories for the same reason.

What's in store next for Felicity, Dougie and co.?

Lots! The prologue to their next adventure is included in this book so do take a look. They have finally persuaded their Dad to take them to France and inevitably they get involved in various unusual goings-on. Our old friend Horsey plays a more prominent role – but he also has a rival! Expect more characters with funny names and lots of excitement. After that further stories will take them to Scotland and Ireland. Watch out for updates on Facebook and Twitter, as well as on the publishing website: www.handbrakepublishing.co.uk

For more information about Glenn Coe please visit his FaceBook page at:
https://www.facebook.com/glenn.coe.108